JUST ONCE

FOR THE LOVE OF THE FLIGHT SERIES

KATHRYN KALEIGH

To learn more about Kathryn Kaleigh, visit

www.kathrynkaleigh.com

Kathryn Kaleigh

CHAPTER 1

The old classic song "Be my Baby" spilled from the jukebox of the Cassville Pizzeria.

It was the perfect background for THE Wynter Jordan and Bradford Cooper engagement party.

The restaurant was currently closed to the public. Unlimited pizza and bottles of ice-cold beer for the dozen or so guests. The bottles of beer were flowing and the pizza was in the oven.

Quiet conversation and laughter wove perfectly into the music.

White rosebuds in silver vases on every table. Sparkly white lights draped from the ceiling, amplifying the festive atmosphere.

Sierra Jordan had taken a table for two on the opposite side of the restaurant from the jukebox. She was currently standing up, though, her back against the wall

She'd grown tired of sitting.

Even in her white canvas sneakers, her swollen feet ached. She shifted from one foot to the other.

She felt overdressed in her ankle-length skirt, but her

long hip-length wool sweater was not only more casual, but kept her warm. She fisted her hands in the pockets and pulled the sweater tightly around her waist.

Sierra's sister Wynter had become reacquainted with her childhood sweetheart, Bradford, just two months ago and now they were planning a Christmas wedding next month.

A wedding that was much overdue.

Sierra and Wynter's parents were here, too, tonight. They'd moved away from Cassville when Sierra was in high school. Rather than deal with Sierra's *issues,* they'd merely moved away from the small town that was accessible only by ferry to the city of Madison.

In the city, Sierra melded into the swirl of other troubled teens. She was barely noticed.

Besides, Sierra had been torn away from her social group and though things hadn't quite settled down, they had changed.

And then there were Bradford's parents. His parents had moved to Florida just months ago with doctor's orders.

That had been a shock to everyone, not the least of all, to Bradford.

The Coopers had run the pizzeria in Cassville forever. At least twenty years. They'd abandoned it, giving Bradford full control over whatever he chose to do with it.

He'd decided to keep it. At least for the time being.

Even though Sierra's parents had driven in this morning and planned to take the late ferry and drive home tonight, Sierra had driven into Cassville herself and booked a room at the hotel.

Things had never completely smoothed out with her parents.

Bradford stood up, Wynter next to him, and lightly tapped a spoon on one of the beer bottles. Both Bradford and Wynter wore huge grins.

Sierra was truly happy for them. She had fond memories of the two of them dating in high school. Before they'd been separated by college.

"I want to thank everyone for making their way here." Bradford put an arm around Wynter and pulled her close. "I know it's not the easiest journey to make. What with the ferry and all."

"Good thing we have a pilot in the family," Mr. Cooper said.

Everyone laughed, knowing that he was talking about his son Bradford.

Sierra smiled. She knew that Bradford had flown down, picked up his parents, and flown them back up to Cassville.

Just for the engagement party tonight.

She envied the closeness of the Coopers.

Nonetheless, she was pleased for her sister.

Sierra sat back down, relieving the pain in her feet.

She'd come to the party by herself. She wasn't intentionally being stand-offish. She'd left Cassville during a turbulent time in her life. Before she formed any lasting friendships, so she didn't really know anyone here other than her family.

And Wynter was the only one she was close to.

Besides, Sierra had decided a few months ago to turn her life around.

And for the foreseeable future that meant staying to herself.

Until June when she was going to be a mother.

With one hand on her baby bump, she looked up and saw *him.*

Her heartrate shot into a staccato rhythm.

CHAPTER 2

Mike Phillips stood at the door of the pizzeria watching his best friend and fiancé as they celebrated their engagement with their family and closest friends.

The Cassville Pizzeria had always been clean and welcoming, but tonight it also looked festive. With its clear twinkling lights and white rose buds.

He was late.

But in his defense, it wasn't his fault.

It was the weather. A thunderstorm had hit just outside of Fort Worth delaying his take off.

He'd made up some of that time during the flight. Thankfully there were no speed limits in the air.

He knew everyone here. Having grown up in Cassville, it was something of a requirement.

Leaning against the closed door, he scanned the familiar faces. There were several people he hadn't seen in quite some time and looked forward to catching up with. Like Mr. and Mrs. Bradford. They'd always been good to him growing up as Bradford's friend.

But when his gaze landed on *her*, he froze.

Sierra Jordan had been much too young for him. Mike was three years older than Bradford. And they were both two years older than Sierra. Five years difference.

Back when he was twenty-one and Sierra had been sixteen, he'd tamped down his attraction to Sierra so fast even he wasn't sure it had actually been real.

If he hadn't memorized her every feature, he wouldn't have recognized her now.

She'd grown up. He did quick math. He was thirty-one. She would be twenty-six herself now.

Her long golden brown hair was styled simply. Straight. With a little curly flip on the ends.

Her lips that had always carried a somewhat impertinent expression, still did.

The song on the jukebox faded into "Waiting for a Girl Like You."

Just as the music changed, Sierra looked up and saw him.

And in that split moment he knew that the attraction for his best friend's little sister that he'd so successfully tamped down had been real. And not so very tamped down as maybe he'd thought.

Bradford spotted him right at that moment, too, and after giving Wynter a quick kiss on the lips, dashed over and gave Mike a big man hug.

"It's great to see you." Bradford had that look that came only from a man truly in love.

"It's been too long." He clapped Bradford on the back. "Skye Travels is growing from what I hear."

"You hear right. Come on." He turned. "Come say hi to Wynter."

Mike walked over to where Wynter stood talking to Bradford's parents.

It was good to see Wynter, too.

But there was really only one girl there tonight that he wanted to talk to.

But how was he supposed to start a conversation with a girl who no doubt thought of him as just a friend of the family?

CHAPTER 3

"Sierra, come get some pizza," Wynter said as she breezed by on her way to speak to someone at a table across from Sierra.

"I will." Sierra waved her off. There was a line right now as Shelley, the pizzeria manager and her two helpers put pizzas out on the counter.

Even though her stomach was grumbling terribly, Sierra didn't want to stand in line.

"Baby it's Cold Outside" was playing on the jukebox now. Despite the controversy surrounding it, it was Sierra's new favorite song.

She loved the happy male-female playfulness of the two vocalists. She may not currently be in a relationship or have any plans to be in a relationship, but she could definitely appreciate the fun of the song.

When Wynter was back at the front table a minute later, Mike leaned over and whispered something to her.

Wynter glanced in her direction and smiled. Sierra's stomach dropped.

Mike had been Bradford's best friend when Sierra still

lived in Cassville. She hadn't seen him since she and her family had moved away just before her junior year.

But she never forgot him and she'd know his laughter anywhere.

He'd been handsome then, but was five years older, and saw her as nothing more than a kid who kept getting into trouble.

He was actually the one who'd gotten her out of trouble and not only was she eternally indebted to him, but it was a secret that the two of them shared.

Mike was thirty-one now. And he was hands down the most handsome man Sierra had ever seen.

He was about six feet tall, not thin, not muscular. Just right. He was clean-shaven with short dark hair. His smile was a bit lop-sided, but when he smiled, his whole face lit up.

She'd had an enormous crush on him back when she was a teenager.

Sierra had watched Mike since the minute she saw him standing at the door. He'd joined Wynter and Bradford at their table and just about everyone had stopped by to say hi to him.

When Mike laughed, every nerve in her body reacted. Even across the room after all these years, when he looked in her direction her pulse shot up dangerously.

The crush, it seemed, had survived the test of time.

Mike went to the counter, put a slice of pizza on each of two plates, then as if on second thought, he picked up two bottles of beer by the neck and headed in her direction.

She held her breath and watched him beneath her eyelashes.

He didn't stop at any of the tables until he got to hers.

He set the beer down first, then the two plates. "Your sister said you like cheese pizza."

Sierra's thoughts scattered into a hundred different directions. She did like cheese pizza.

But Mike Phillips delivering pizza to her table was something she never would have even imagined.

"Do you mind if I join you?"

He didn't wait for an answer, but sat down opposite her and slid a plate of pizza and a beer in front of her.

She stared blankly at him.

"I'm Mike," he said with a grin.

Sierra laughed before she could catch herself. "Hello Mike."

She could tell he was a little caught off balance – not quite certain that she remembered him. Him being off balance, oddly enough, put her a bit back into balance.

"Thank you," she said, picking up her bottle of water and drinking.

Studying her, he bit into his slice of pizza. "How have you been?"

"Good," she said, then she picked up her own slice of pizza and bit into it. She closed her eyes. The pizza here was heavenly.

When she opened her eyes, Mike was grinning at her.

She blushed.

"Beer?" He picked up one of the bottles.

Sierra shook her head.

Mike shrugged. And tipped his beer bottle back for a drink. "It's about time these two got back together, huh?"

Sierra smiled. "Agreed." Her feet were uncomfortable again. She would feel much better out of her shoes and in her slippers.

She'd sometimes imagined meeting Mike again. Somewhere.

But after they moved away from Cassville and Wynter

and Bradford broke up, she'd given up on seeing him again. Bradford was her last link to Mike.

And here she was back in Cassville.

Wynter and Bradford back together.

With Mike sitting right in front of her.

The difference was she was no longer the troubled teen she'd been when she last saw him.

Oddly enough though, the age difference that prevented her even pretending to herself that he might be interested was no longer an issue.

"Penny for your thoughts." He'd finished off his slice of pizza and was leaning forward, his elbows on the table.

She shook off her reverie and blinked at the man – the real man – in front of her.

He was even more handsome than she remembered.

And her attraction was even stronger.

"I was just thinking how odd it is to be back in Cassville. It's almost like taking a trip back in time." She looked toward her sister, smiling with Bradford. "With my sister and all."

Mike reached out and picked up the little heart she wore on a chain around her neck. "Oh. I think plenty of time has passed." He dropped the necklace and leaned back in his chair, his gaze still locked on hers.

A pain shot through Sierra's stomach, reminding her that time had indeed passed.

And Mike was even more off limits than he had been before.

CHAPTER 4

ike's cell phone rang and he reluctantly tore himself away from Sierra. He let the call go to voice mail just long enough for him to excuse himself and step outside.

"I have to take this call," he said.

She shrugged. "I'm sure I'll see you around."

"Yeah." At least until after the wedding next month. He picked up their plates, his empty beer bottle and her full one, realizing she hadn't even touched her alcohol.

The wild child, it seemed had done some settling down.

He stepped outside into the fresh cool air and returned his phone call, pacing down the path toward Bradford's house. His parents' house actually, though they now lived in Florida.

Ten minutes later, he turned and started back. Some of the guests were leaving now.

He picked up his pace, hoping to catch another glimpse of Sierra before she left.

He stepped back into the warmth of the pizzeria. The juke box was quiet now and the place was almost empty.

He saw Sierra, her back to him, talking to Wynter. Sierra was wearing a black hip-length wool coat with a light gray scarf. After quickly hugging her sister, Sierra turned.

Mike had been about to step forward. To say whatever inane thing popped into his head, when he froze.

Now he knew why Sierra hadn't touched her beer.

She had one hand on her stomach, swollen just enough for him to know.

She was expecting.

Whatever hopes and dreams he'd unconsciously entertained shattered and fell at his feet.

If she was pregnant, that meant that she wasn't available.

Somehow that scenario hadn't occurred to him.

A big part of him still saw her as a teenager.

But he shifted his thoughts, accepting that she was all grown up.

She stepped forward to stand in front of him. "It's good to see you, Mike." There was a wistfulness in her tone. She must have seen the surprise – the shock – on his face.

He glanced at her hands. She wasn't wearing a ring. "It's good to see you, too." And he meant it. He'd thought about her a lot. Too much. Just knowing she was out there somewhere in the world had made him feel better.

She walked past him and a sudden panic swept over him. Whatever her situation was, if she walked out that door, there was very little chance that he would get another opportunity to talk with her.

There would be the wedding of course. But weddings were always chaotic and he couldn't count on getting a chance then. She might not even come to the wedding alone.

He turned just as she passed. "Wait. Sierra."

She turned back. Her face was flushed prettily and he realized that's what they meant when they said pregnant women glowed. "Can I walk you out?"

She didn't answer at first and he was sure that she was going to say no. Instead she said. "Sure."

He grinned again. He would have a few more minutes with the grown-up version of the teenage girl he'd crushed on when he was just a little too old for her.

They stepped out into the cool air and she shuddered.

"Where are you parked?" he asked.

"I walked. I'm staying at the hotel."

"It's a good night for a walk." He fell into step beside her. "It'll be snowing soon."

She nodded. "Cassville's pretty in the winter."

"Since you're at the hotel, I'm guessing you didn't move back here."

"I live in Madison. You?" She looked at him from the corner of her eye.

"I'm in Dallas."

"Right." Their footsteps crunched over the fallen oak leaves on the sidewalk. Mike missed the smell of northern winters.

"You're still a pilot?" she asked.

He shrugged. "Flying gets in the blood. I'm not sure I could stop if I had to."

A sadness swept over her features. He didn't like it. He wanted to destroy whatever it was that had put that sadness on her face.

"Don't I know?" she said. "I was a flight attendant until…." She nodded toward her abdomen.

Mike stopped. Then his face broke into a wide grin. "You're one of us."

"No." She shook her head. "I quit. And I won't be going back."

CHAPTER 5

The air smelled like snow. It was crisp and clean. There was nothing like seeing those first snowflakes of the season.

The cold air felt good to her skin. And walking felt even better.

A dog barked in the distance, but otherwise it was quiet. Different background noise than Madison.

Sierra kept walking. She hadn't planned on telling Mike anything about herself. Her life.

But she'd always trusted him. He was easy to talk to. And he'd kept her secret all this time.

Still. She'd promised herself that she wouldn't get close to anyone else.

She needed to straighten out her life and get ready to be a mother.

It was taking all her energy. She wanted to stay settled. To not get hurt again.

Mike took two long strides and caught up with her. "Seriously? You were a flight attendant? Which airline?"

"A small private company." She didn't tell him that she'd gotten mixed up with the owner's son.

That was something she would never tell anyone.

Her life had far too many secrets.

And Mike already knew one. He didn't need to know just how off track she'd gotten.

She'd started over and she was determined to keep it that way.

A new life.

"What are you doing now?" he asked.

Again. More secrets.

But this particular secret was one she nourished and protected. So she evaded his question. "I'm taking some time off."

"What about the father?"

She glanced at him sideways. Mike had never been one to avoid the hard topics.

She took a deep breath. This was one question she'd prepared herself for. "We're not together." It was the simplest answer she had been able to come up with.

She'd even told Wynter – her own sister – that she didn't know who the father was. She was afraid of what Wynter might do. Her sister was all about people taking responsibility for their actions.

"I'm sorry," Mike said, giving the typical answer. Then he gave the Mike answer. "Sometimes that's for the best."

"Yes," she said as they turned down the sidewalk toward the hotel. "Sometimes it is."

"When are you leaving town?"

They stood at the door to the hotel lobby, facing each other. The evening wind swirled her hair into her face. She swept it back. "Sometime in the morning."

"Can I buy you breakfast?"

Her heart answered before her brain had time to engage. "I'd like that."

He grinned. "I'll meet you in the lobby at what? Seven? Eight?"

"Eight sounds good."

He put a hand on her cheek and kissed her forehead. "Sleep well my little one." Then he turned and walked down the sidewalk. She didn't want him to leave. It seemed like every step tugged that much more at her heartstrings.

When he reached the corner, she went inside the lobby.

After the door closed behind her, she turned and looked back one more time.

Mike was standing there. Waiting for her to go inside.

He had been her protector when she was a teenager.

And now she realized he was a piece of the puzzle that she'd been trying to figure out.

Maybe one day everything would sort itself out and make sense.

Until then, she had tomorrow to look forward to.

CHAPTER 6

After Sierra went inside, Mike stood there, the wind swirling around him, sweeping leaves from the oak trees.

He could still smell the scent of lavender in Sierra's hair and felt the softness of her skin on his fingertips.

Mike was staying at the hotel, too. It was the only decent place in town. But he didn't say anything to Sierra.

He wasn't ready to go inside yet.

He needed to take a walk. To think.

There was so much information that he needed to process.

First of all, Sierra wasn't sixteen any more. She'd grown up and grown up beautifully.

Sierra was also an expectant mother. The father wasn't in the picture. But unless modern technology was involved, there had been someone.

She lived in Madison.

That was all he knew about her.

It was just enough information to put him in a tailspin. Not enough to get him leveled out.

Mike had never been married, but was something of a serial dater. He didn't play the field so to speak. He'd have a girlfriend, then maybe another, but when things started to get serious, he'd duck out and take a break.

He'd been called commitment phobic. Along with a few other things.

But the way he saw it, the life of a pilot didn't really set the foundation for a serious relationship.

It was an excuse and he admitted it.

Especially now, seeing Bradford so happy with Wynter. Bradford had even managed to talk Noah Worthington – the up and coming entrepreneur of the century – into basing a plane in Madison.

Bradford wasn't worrying – at least not visibly – about what his job might do to his marriage. He seemed confident that whatever it was, he and Wynter were strong enough to handle it.

Mike stopped at the park in the middle of town square in the middle of Main Street.

His pulse was still beating a little faster than normal. He felt like he'd just pulled out of a downward spiral.

He hadn't felt this way after talking to a girl since Mary Belle Harris had asked him to the Sadie Hawkins dance senior year.

Mike laughed at himself. It was funny how being back in his hometown brought back so many memories of his youth.

Especially since he'd left for Auburn University right after high school graduation and hadn't been back. He'd graduated college and gone to work for himself. He couldn't imagine what it would be like to follow someone else's schedule and hoped he never had to find out.

Right now he worked an average of four days a week. Sometimes he'd spend a weekend or even a week at his client's destinations. It was easier for them to pay for him to stay with them than it was to have him come and go.

He'd been so many places. Aspen. Vegas. Bahamas. St. Pete Beach. He liked the Rocky Mountains best. If he ever took a vacation of his own choosing, that's where he'd go. Maybe Vail or Estes Park. He'd get a cabin by a stream.

He stared at the really old oak tree in the center of the square. It was now considered a protected tree and no one could cut it down.

He pulled himself back from the path his thoughts had taken him.

In his little vacation world, Sierra was at the cabin with him, sitting in a rocker on the front porch, a baby in her arms.

Mike was in a world of trouble.

CHAPTER 7

Sierra stepped off the elevator to the third floor – the top floor – and made her way to her room.

Someone on the floor had popped popcorn. The scent made Sierra's stomach queasy. Most everything did these days.

At least it was warm inside. For the moment at any rate. And quiet. It didn't take much noise to give her a pounding headache.

She blissfully stepped out of her sneakers and laid crossways on the queen-sized bed.

She could get so tired she could barely move. Like right now.

Maybe she would just take a nap in her clothes. She could change later.

She wrapped the quilt around her and hugged a pillow to her chest.

Warm and cozy now, she stared at the white ceiling and let her mind wander.

It immediately wandered to Mike. The object of her teenage fantasies.

But he'd been her brother's friend and was much too old for her. Nonetheless, he'd been kind. He'd been the one she'd called when she needed help the most.

She hadn't thought she'd ever see him again.

Then he was standing at the pizzeria door. Looking almost the same. Like her fantasies come to life. He was wearing dark gray slacks and a white shirt beneath a dark gray overcoat. His dark hair had a touch of gray to it now, but it only added to his good looks.

She'd heard his laughter across the room, setting every nerve on fire.

But when he'd sat across from her bearing pizza and beer, he'd looked at her *that* way. Sierra told herself she was imagining things, but she was the wild girl. The girl who knew the way a man looked at a woman when he was attracted to her.

Mike was attracted to her.

Even if on the outside chance she was mistaken, she'd sworn off men for the foreseeable future. Her focus was on being a good mother. Nothing else.

She needed to keep herself on the straight and narrow path. Mike Phillips was not a straight and narrow guy.

Not for her anyway.

For Sierra, Mike was oh-so-much danger.

Her first instinct had been to hide her pregnancy from him. But there was no hiding it. And no reason to. With him still being friends with Bradford, he'd find out anyway. And she'd definitely be showing by the time her sister's wedding came around next month.

Once he had time to think about it, he'd no longer be attracted to her anyway.

No man in his right mind would want to date a girl who was already pregnant.

Especially not Mike Phillips.

CHAPTER 8

The next morning at a quarter to eight, Mike stepped out of the elevator door to the scent of strong coffee and doughnuts.

He never understood why anyone would want to eat sugar biscuits for breakfast. He was a bacon and egg kind of guy.

The Weather Channel was on in the lobby not surprisingly predicting snow. The clerk behind the desk was taking a reservation.

Sierra sat on one of the hotel lobby's two couches. She expected him to come in through the front door, so when Mike came in through the other side of the lobby, he just stopped.

And watched her. She was bundled in her black wool coat, a red scarf around her neck. She was wearing jeans and her legs bounced up and down.

She chewed on her thumb nail for a moment, then tucked her hands in her pockets.

Mike hadn't been sure Sierra would actually meet him for breakfast. But she was there. She was early. And she was nervous.

He took all those things as good signs.

He saw the surprise on her face when she glanced in his direction and saw him. She quickly tried to cover it with a smile. Also nervous.

He grinned.

Reaching her side, he held out a hand and pulled her to her feet. He hugged her close. After a moment's hesitation, she hugged him back, resting her cheek on his chest. He rested his chin on the top of her head. Like yesterday, her hair smelled like lavender.

"Good morning, Little One," he said, releasing her.

"Good morning." Her cheeks were flushed and her eyes a bit misty. She looked tired with dark circles under her eyes. She'd used concealer so they were only visible up close.

"Are you ok?" A jolt of alarm shot through him. Mike had never dated a pregnant woman and knew very little about what to expect. His sister had a three-year-old, but she lived in Europe and he'd only seen the baby once.

Sierra nodded, tucking her hands back in her pockets. "The cold air."

There was no cold air at the moment, but Mike let it slide. "I hope you're hungry."

"Starving." She shrugged. "But that's subject to change at any given minute."

"Really?" Mike took her arm and tucked it through his. "That must be annoying."

She laughed. "You have no idea."

He held the door open for her to walk outside first. A blast of cold air hit them in the face. "Now that's cold."

She shivered. "Are we walking?"

"It's not far." He was taking her to a little diner across the street. Unlike the hotel, they had real food.

They stood at the curb and waited for the traffic to clear.

He took her arm again. It wasn't something he normally did, but it seemed appropriate to escort her. He didn't know if it was because he still thought of her as being a teen or if it was because she was pregnant. Or something else. At any rate, she seemed fragile.

Someone in a pickup truck waved as they passed.

"Is that someone you…" Mike looked over at Sierra.

She was white as a sheet.

CHAPTER 9

The sleepy little town of Cassville had surprisingly heavy traffic this early in the morning. Three pickup trucks. A couple of cars, one with loud music pounding from it.

She could smell the food from the diner across the two-lane street. It was a small diner that had been there forever. She couldn't remember ever eating there, though. Her parents tended to keep their two girls at home. After they moved to Madison, her dad started bringing home take-out most every night. By then Sierra was rarely home.

She'd moved out the day after her eighteenth birthday and went to work as a clerk at a supermarket. That was before she met Jeff.

Sierra was so cold, her nose felt numb.

The crisp air brought tears to her eyes. Cold air always did that to her, so it was a good excuse for being teary-eyed.

She'd hadn't been completely truthful with Mike earlier. She'd been teary-eyed from thinking about how under different circumstances, she would have been excited to be meeting Mike for breakfast.

Not that she hadn't been excited, but this was a different kind of excitement. This was a what could have been excitement rather than a what might be kind of excitement.

She'd slept fitfully last night leaving dark circles under her eyes this morning. She'd dabbed on a little concealer and she was good to go.

She kept waking up with dreams about Mike. She used to do that years ago, but she'd stopped. She used to think of it as him visiting her in her sleep.

She'd never told anyone that, not even her counselor. She didn't want to have to be hospitalized for delusions or hallucinations or whatever it was they might decide to call it.

But right now she was in some kind of daze. Walking arm in arm with Mike was surreal. It was so outlandish, it wasn't something she'd even imagined in her wildest fantasies.

When the bright blue pickup truck slowed, her first instinct was to step back, but Mike held her in place with his arm.

Then she recognized the truck. A shot of fear shot through her.

But it wasn't him. It wasn't Jeff.

Jeff would never show up in Cassville. He probably didn't even know where to find it on a map.

Nonetheless, Mike had seen her reaction.

She shook her head. "No. I don't know him."

"Are you sure?" Mike asked as the truck straightened and passed them by without incident.

"I thought I recognized the truck, but it wasn't… I was mistaken." She tried to smile, but wasn't sure it was much more than a lip wobble.

She thought she'd put Jeff out of her mind. But just seeing a pickup truck that resembled his sent her into such a panic, that she wasn't sure what to think.

She had about one hour with Mike and she was determined to make the most of it.

CHAPTER 10

$\mathcal{M}$ ike watched the tail lights of the blue pickup truck until it disappeared down the street, lost in the light traffic.

He'd held Sierra's arm, prepared to pull her away from danger as the truck slowed and veered too close.

He must have seen the truck's wheels straighten before Sierra did.

The look on her face wasn't one of fear. It was something else. Recognition maybe.

He'd caught a glimpse of the driver as the truck passed them. It was a young man, maybe early twenties.

But she said she was mistaken.

Despite his instinct telling him differently, he had to go with what she said.

Whether she knew him or not wasn't really the point.

The point was that Sierra was fragile. She was strong, too, of course, but she was also fragile.

She presented that persona of strength to the world. But beneath that strength, she was like fine glass. Glass that could shatter into a million pieces.

She'd always been fragile, though he wasn't sure if anyone else really saw her that way.

Mike had seen through the brave front she presented to the world when she was only sixteen.

He'd helped her then and he'd help her now.

If he could figure out how.

CHAPTER 11

$\mathcal{M}$ ike sat across from her in a booth in the little diner that smelled like grease – in a good way.

He sat with his elbows on the table, a goofy little sideways smile on his face. Just staring at her with those bright blue eyes.

There were so many items on the menu, that Sierra quickly got overwhelmed. So many things sounded alike. And she couldn't focus with Mike watching her. She shifted in her seat, trying to get comfortable. Her feet hurt even in her broken-in sneakers. If she was at home, she'd have her feet up on the ottoman.

When Mike ordered two eggs over-easy, bacon, and hashbrowns, she looked at him with relief and asked to have the same.

After the server left them alone, Sierra leaned back and met Mike's gaze. She'd built a whole fantasy world around him, but she realized suddenly that she knew next to nothing about the real man. The one sitting in front of her.

She couldn't fathom why he'd asked her to breakfast.

"How far along are you?" he asked out of the blue.

She blinked and felt a little flush on her cheeks. "Twelve weeks." She had to admit she felt self-conscious about Mike knowing she was pregnant.

She always imagined when – if – she saw him again, she'd look her best. Being pregnant was not looking her best.

"Wow. You're showing early."

She was flushing now. She picked up her glass and sipped cool water through a straw. "My doctor says it's probably because I'm so thin."

He grinned. "It's cute."

She set her glass down and closed her eyes.

This was a bad idea. She should have stayed safely in the hotel room. Actually she should be driving herself home now. Either way, she should most definitely not be sitting here in a booth in a diner in Cassville. Across from Mike.

"Here."

She opened her eyes.

He patted the booth next to him. "Put your feet up here."

She shook her head.

He looked at her sideways. "Humor me. Let me feel like I'm helping."

She blew out a breath, but shrugged and put her feet up on the booth.

He grinned. "Better?"

She sighed. "You must know a lot about expecting women." As soon as the words were out of her mouth, she looked at him. This is where he would tell her he had three kids and two ex-wives. And was working on a third wife.

"I know absolutely nothing at all."

She tilted her head to the side. He had to be teasing her.

"My sister has a three-year-old," he said, "but she lives in Europe and I've only seen the baby one time."

Maybe he wasn't teasing her. She took a deep breath and found the strength to ask. "What about your own children?"

He looked a little green around the gills. For just a moment. He shook his head. "No children."

She knew the follow-up question involved wives. But she couldn't bring herself to ask out loud. It was enough to know right now that he didn't have children.

And he wasn't wearing a ring.

She was saved by the server who brought their food.

She took a bite of crispy bacon. Some hashbrowns. Then she cut into the egg setting a burst of yellow liquid across her plate.

She put a hand on her throat.

So much for making the most of her hour with Mike.

"I'm going to be sick."

CHAPTER 12

When Sierra said she was going to be sick, she meant she was going to be sick right now. This second.

Her eyes wide, she turned to her right, bent over, and everything came up.

The server rushed over. Mike tamped down his inner panic and asked the server to bring some towels and a clean damp cloth.

He scooted over to her side of the booth and put a hand on her back.

The server was back with a damp cloth. "It's clean," she assured him. "And here are some towels. But I'll clean it up." Then she left them alone.

Sierra straightened and took the damp cloth from him. Wiped her mouth.

She kept her eyes down.

"Are you alright?" Mike asked.

She shook her head.

The bolt of panic that he thought he had under control broke free and shot through him. "What is it? The baby?"

She shook her head. Put a hand over her eyes. "I need…" She put the cloth over her mouth. "I need out. Please."

"Of course." Mike slid out of the booth.

Sierra slid out behind him and rushed away.

He assumed she was headed to the restroom.

He sat back down on his side of the booth and the server came over to clean up the mess.

The server asked him something, but he didn't catch what it was. Instead, he watched helplessly as Sierra went out the diner door and raced across the street.

He pulled out his money clip and left what was probably twice what the breakfast cost lying on the table.

By the time he got to the door, Sierra was inside the hotel doors across the street.

He stepped out into the cold and just stood there.

Cars passed this way and that. People came and went through the diner door.

He barely even noticed them.

CHAPTER 13

*S*ierra looked over her shoulder as she unlocked her car door. She was panting from the little jog she'd taken across the street.

Shivering inside the car, she turned on the heat full blast. She leaned her head against the steering wheel for just a minute.

She'd checked out and rolled her suitcase down to the car before she'd met Mike for breakfast.

Driving out of the hotel parking lot, she looked around for Mike, but didn't see him anywhere. She headed toward the ferry.

She was a coward.

She'd wanted to have a nice breakfast with Mike. To present herself as an adult who had things together now. Unlike when she was a teen.

Instead, she'd thrown up at the breakfast table. In the restaurant. Right in front of him.

Her cheeks were flushed with embarrassment. She was humiliated.

She told herself she couldn't help it. It was the pregnancy.

But it didn't matter. She couldn't face him again.

There was her sister's wedding next month, but she'd figure something out. Maybe she wouldn't be able to go.

She stopped and waited in the parking lot for the ferry.

Of course she wanted to be at her sister's wedding. She just didn't want to see Mike. Maybe he wouldn't be there.

She'd have to worry about that later.

Right now, all she wanted to do was to get home and bury her head beneath her blankets.

She watched the road in her rearview mirror. Halfway expecting Mike to follow her.

But he didn't.

She'd done the grown-up thing all right.

She'd run away.

CHAPTER 14

One Month Later

The little white chapel in the heart of Cassville was filled with white candles. Chunky candles. Tall thin candles.

On the window ledges. At the prayer desk. At the altar. All glowing with soft flames.

Everything was red or white. White candles. Red bows.

A formally dressed trio group – two guys and one girl – college students – played slow, romantic music.

Sierra adjusted her solid red organza dress. The empire waistband of the dress wrapped around her, tying into a big bow at her back.

She took the box holding a red and white bouquet from the delivery boy and carried it back to the dressing area. The bouquet was late. Wynter had done a good job of not panicking.

But surprisingly enough, everything had come together.

Wynter was alone now. Everyone else had been seated.

Sierra stopped in the doorway and just stared at her big

sister. Wynter's strapless mermaid style wedding dressing set off her figure perfectly.

Sierra ran a hand self-consciously over her little baby bump. She wondered if she'd ever have that kind of figure again. Just in the off chance that she wanted to get married some day.

Wynter's red taffeta dress had a white underskirt and a white band at the waist. The white on her dress – along with the elegance of the gown – set her apart from Sierra and their mom.

It was a small wedding, just family and a few close friends, but Wynter wanted pictures. And pictures required formal dresses.

"Wynter," Sierra's eyes were damp. "I've never seen you look so beautiful."

"Well… I've never been a bride before." Wynter smiled, her skin glowing.

"You should have."

Wynter laughed. "Probably. But it wasn't my time." She stepped forward and took the flower box from Sierra.

"Now is definitely your time."

"Oh, Sierra, your time will come." Wynter opened the box and gently lifted the bouquet to sniff the dewy red roses.

Sierra sat on a little cloth stool, letting her feet rest a moment. She was grateful that she was wearing only little one-inch heels. "It's not about me. I don't even care about getting married.

Wynter turned and looked at her. "Of course you do." Her gaze strayed to Sierra's abdomen.

"I don't need the complications. I want to just raise my baby alone."

"That's hard. Remember how Uncle Jamie raised his son himself?"

Sierra did remember. Their mom's brother had spent

several months living with them after his wife passed during childbirth.

It had pretty much taken the whole family those first few months to care for the baby. Sierra and Wynter had been children themselves – twelve and ten – but they'd been enlisted to help out, too.

Sierra had vivid memories of heating bottles and changing diapers.

She figured she had a better foundation for raising a baby than a lot of mothers.

Nonetheless, she had no delusions about it being easy. Not the pregnancy, the childbirth, or the years after the baby was born.

Years.

Sierra actually believed that life as she knew it was over.

She'd never date again.

Oddly enough, she didn't really mind. Sierra had done her share of dating. She was ready to move to something different. Something meaningful.

Raising a child was meaningful.

She hoped.

"We have to go," Wynter said as the clock tolled the hour.

Sierra and Wynter walked arm-in-arm to the back door of the chapel.

Looking up, she saw that she was face-to-face with Mike.

CHAPTER 15

Mike caught his breath when Sierra stepped up to the door. Her long hair was pulled atop her head and fell in loose curls over her left shoulder.

She was beautiful in a floor-length solid red dress with an empire waist.

With her holding Wynter's bouquet in front of her, no one would know that she was pregnant just by looking.

A flash of guilty hope shot threw him at the thought that maybe she was no longer pregnant. Then she took a step and he saw her baby bump.

It was a normal reaction, he told himself to want her to be the way he'd imagined her all these years.

Unencumbered. And available.

She'd implied that she was available. But Mike was a bit confused on that point.

They hadn't explored anything beyond her saying that the baby's father wasn't in her life.

There were other possibilities that he had to consider. With Sierra, he couldn't rule anything out.

She was one of the most fascinating people he'd ever known. She had so many layers. So much personality.

She'd gone from troubled teen to settled woman.

A woman he wanted to get to know.

No one had told him he'd be walking down the aisle with her. And from the look on her face, no one had bothered to tell her either. As far as he knew, no one knew of their… past. He wasn't sure what he'd call it. Friendship? History?

He held out his arm and she linked hers with his. He put his hand over hers. In just a month's time, her skin seemed to have gotten even softer. And she was even more beautiful.

She looked like a princess in her red gown. She even looked pretty as a bride herself.

The Christmas red dress accented the flush on her cheeks. Her lips were red, whether from lipstick or pregnancy, he didn't know, and glossy.

And she smelled good like she always did. Like lavender this time. A soft scent. Not a harsh perfumy scent so many women wore.

A month had passed since he'd seen her. He'd thought about trying to find her. A lot. All he had to do was ask Bradford for her number or address. It would have been easy to come up with some excuse to see her.

But he'd gone with his instinct and given her space and time. He knew he'd see her today.

He hadn't known that his best friend and bride would pair them up so conveniently.

The wedding march began and the two of them started down the aisle.

Mike was reminded that it was a small wedding and they were the only ones coming down the aisle other than the bride.

He felt his own skin flush with both Wynter's and

Bradford's families watching them walk down the aisle together.

She looked up at him. His pulse hitched as her green eyes locked onto his.

His imagination strayed to walking down the aisle with Sierra.

With her as the bride. For them to be married.

He looked away from her siren green eyes and kept his gaze straight ahead.

He needed to pull himself together.

He was feeling like a besotted teenager.

CHAPTER 16

What had Wynter done?

She'd paired Sierra and Mike together. To walk down the aisle together.

And she hadn't bothered to even so much as mention it.

She glanced enviously at the trio playing the wedding march. They had a job to do. A purpose.

Besides, in her opinion, they were doing an excellent job.

Sierra was pleased with her sister's choice in music. It didn't matter that the only people there were their families and a few close friends.

It was a celebratory occasion for the two of them. And their friends and families as well.

As far as Sierra was concerned, it was quality, not quantity. She'd come a long way since her party days in the not nearly far enough past. Back in those days, a gathering like this wouldn't have interested her much.

Other than Mike being here.

She'd always been interested when Mike was around.

She'd thought about contacting him to apologize for the way she'd run off after their breakfast last month.

Wynter would have given her his phone number. In fact, Sierra could have looked it up on the internet herself. All she'd have had to do is google his name. Being a private pilot with his own business, he'd be out there.

She'd actually been impressed with her restraint in not looking him up.

She'd known she would see him here at the wedding. But she certainly hadn't thought she'd be walking down the aisle on his arm.

If she hadn't wanted to keep her… friendship with Mike private, she'd be all over Wynter for not telling her about this ahead of time.

But, she pasted a smile on her face. The last thing she wanted to do was put a damper on her sister's wedding.

The wedding march began signaling them to start down the aisle.

Sierra's heart did summersaults all over the place.

She was walking down the aisle with Mike Phillips. It was like her teenage fantasy coming to life.

Except Mike was looking straight ahead, his expression showing consternation.

Her world was suddenly spinning. Her one-inch heels were too high and she swayed, grabbing hold of Mike's arm.

He stopped, grabbed both her arms, and steadied her. "Are you ok?"

She looked up, their gazes locking. She saw genuine concern now.

"I'm ok." She steadied herself and smiled reassuringly at the few concerned faces who happened to have seen her misstep.

Fortunately, most eyes were on Wynter now, as they should be. Her sister was a beautiful princess in her red and white gown.

They kept walking, his hold on her arm tightened. She drew in deep calming breaths.

It was just Mike. It was just her sister's wedding.

Not hers.

They reached the front of the church where they had to split up to stand on their respective sides.

He looked into her eyes. "Will you be ok?" She saw so much compassion, it made her eyes tear.

She blinked rapidly. And nodded.

She was going to be alright.

She wasn't so sure about her heart.

CHAPTER 17

The wedding was beautiful. At least what Mike saw of it.

It was touching to watch his best friend from childhood wed his high school sweetheart. Bradford and Wynter were so ridiculously in love, it was almost painful to watch.

The scent of her bouquet of red and white roses filled the air. White candles scattered around the little chapel provided a lovely backdrop to her red wedding gown.

Whoever would have thought a bride would wear red to her own wedding? But Wynter pulled it off beautifully.

But it was her little sister, Sierra, who stole Mike's attention. The little sister was all grown up now and to his eyes, even more beautiful than the bride. He would never ever tell anyone that though. It would be the biggest faux pas.

Except maybe Sierra.

He might tell her one day.

She glanced at him and caught him staring at her. He smiled.

She tore her gaze away, a delicate flush sweeping across her cheeks.

Just when he'd convinced himself to think about something else, she'd nearly fell into his arms.

And he was right back where he started.

Besotted.

CHAPTER 18

After the wedding at the little chapel, everyone had walked back to the pizzeria. Wynter and Bradford went first, then the little wedding party – Sierra and Mike, then the families and guests.

The photographer tagged along taking wedding pictures here and there.

Sierra's nose was still cold from the slow two-block walk from the chapel.

She picked up a glass of fruit punch, sniffed it, and pushed it across the table. She didn't smell any alcohol, but she couldn't be too cautious. Weddings were notorious for having spiked punch.

Instead, she picked up her water bottle and drank deeply.

The wedding had brought up a whole spectrum of emotions. Sierra was proud of her sister for so many reasons. She was proud that she'd given her high school love a second chance. So many wouldn't.

For Sierra, the wedding was also bittersweet. It was a little bit humiliating that she wasn't married and it was obvious that she was one who was pregnant.

She pushed the thought away as she'd learned to do.

It had taken quite a bit of mental resetting to come out in public with her head held high. Whenever she found herself in that frame of mind, she reminded herself there were a lot of women who had babies without a husband. For so many reasons.

Sierra never entertained the thought of not having the baby. As the weeks went by, she was becoming more and more attached to the little boy or girl that rode along with her wherever she went.

She also never entertained, as least not seriously, the idea of telling the baby's father. He was engaged now, so he'd lost the privilege of knowing that he was about to be the father of her baby.

Ironically, she learned of his engagement the same day she found out she was pregnant. That was a clear sign if ever she saw one.

But all these thoughts that she'd been dealing with for months now paled in the light of Mike's presence.

Mike being here. Looking at her like that. Changed everything.

He'd watched her during the ceremony more than he'd watched Wynter and Bradford. No one else knew. He'd been standing so that anyone else would have thought he was dutifully watching the happy couple.

But Sierra had felt his gaze on her. His gaze was warm, like sunshine.

And like sunshine, it brought a glow to her cheeks and a smile to her lips.

Even though she'd bit her lip, trying not to smile, while Wynter and Bradford promised to love each other through sickness and health, the smile had come through her eyes. She felt it each time she allowed herself to glance in Mike's direction.

She set the half empty water bottle aside just as Mike slid out the chair next to hers and sat down.

He didn't even bother asking anymore. She didn't let herself think about it too much.

And she certainly didn't allow herself to get used to it. Mike was a free-spirited kind of guy. He'd be here today, then tomorrow he'd be flying off somewhere else.

"I'd like you to meet someone," Mike slid a piece of cake in her direction.

"Who's that?" She eyed the cake speculatively wondering which would come first – the cake or the someone he wanted her to meet.

Mike grinned and sampled the cake. "This is actually good cake."

"I know." Sierra grinned. "I helped her choose it."

"Good job." Mike swirled his fork across the icing. "Two people actually. Noah and Savannah Worthington."

Sierra held her fork in mid-air, halfway to the cake. "Not THE Noah Worthington?" Noah Worthington of Skye Travels had taken on legendary status. She'd heard so much about him since Wynter had gotten back together with Bradford.

Both Bradford and Mike worked for Noah, though Mike just did some occasional contract work. He didn't work a regular week like Bradford. At least that's what Bradford had told them.

Mike nodded. "They were at the wedding. There was something they had to do, but they're planning to stop by before they fly out."

"Wow." She didn't know what to say. But she was suddenly nervous.

Not because she was going to be meeting Noah Worthington.

But because she was going to be meeting one of Mike's colleagues.

CHAPTER 19

Someone had turned on the jukebox and Michael Buble was singing a Christmas song.

The pizzeria was filled mostly with the same people who'd been at the engagement party last month along with a few other guests.

Tonight though, instead of beer and pizza, they had champagne and wedding cake. Wedding cake that was actually edible. Mike couldn't remember ever having decent cake at a wedding.

The song got stuck in Mike's head and he couldn't help wondering how he was going to get Sierra to spend more time with him over the next couple of days.

He'd purposely kept his schedule free for this very reason.

But then he could do that anytime he wanted to.

Christmas was in two days and Mike had nothing to do. No family. His parents had been gone years ago and he was an only child.

Mike wanted Sierra to meet Noah. He wanted to be able to show her off. He wanted her to be with him.

The best way he could figure out to do that was to

monopolize her time and introduce her to his world as the opportunity came up. When he saw Noah and his wife at the wedding, he'd decided right then that that was a good place to start.

Then he could work his way down.

Maybe by the end of the evening, he'd start introducing her as his girlfriend. He knew he could get away with it just because Sierra saw him as a guy who would spontaneously do that sort of thing and not mean a thing by it.

Sometimes that would be an accurate way to describe the things he did.

But not tonight. Tonight he actually meant it.

He was surprised that it didn't bother him that she was pregnant. Especially with someone else's baby.

He'd have to figure that out later. Right now, he didn't question it. He just went with his instinct to protect her.

Someone had not taken proper care of her.

All in all, it was probably better if he didn't know who the father was. Not knowing kept him from looking the guy up and knocking a few teeth out. Mike was a bit of a scrapper in his youth and he wasn't above a good fight now and then. Sometimes it was what a guy needed to be put in line.

It would have been hard knowing who'd left her to fend for herself and not put his hands on the guy. It didn't even matter if she had been the one to decide they weren't together.

Whatever the reason, he didn't like it that someone had put his girl in harm's way.

His girl.

Besotted.

CHAPTER 20

There was one word to describe Savannah Worthington. Charming.

Beautiful. Poised. Elegant.

But above all, charming.

"Anytime you're in Texas, you're welcome to come for a visit." Savannah looked from Sierra to Mike who stood at her side. "Even if Mike isn't with you."

Sierra looked questioningly up at Mike. What had he told his boss and his wife Savannah?

He had used her name to introduce her, not specifying any kind of relationship. But the way he was standing next to her felt like something.

"Thank you." Sierra smiled, laughing at herself. She was the one trying to define in relationship terms what was no more than a friendship. A ten-year friendship, but most of that time, they hadn't even known where the other was.

Now that she thought about it, she was surprised that he even remembered her. They hadn't dated. He'd been too old for her. He'd been an adult with a life – a job and girlfriends…

Although she couldn't remember him ever having a girlfriend.

She looked at him sideways. Did he even like girls?

A little touch of panic shot through her and she swayed.

Mike took her elbow. "We're gonna just sit down for a minute."

He gently led her to the nearest available chair. "Are you ok?"

Sierra sat and took a deep steadying breath. "I'm so sorry."

"It's not your fault." Mike glanced toward her baby bump.

Right. She kept forgetting why her emotions were all over the place. It wasn't the wedding. It was the pregnancy.

It wasn't even Mike.

There weren't any other chairs available, so he knelt next to her and looked into her eyes.

Or was it?

CHAPTER 21

*I*n some form or fashion, at least in his head, Sierra had always been his girl.

Mike had learned not to question such insights. He just let them be what they would.

Noah Worthington looked over as though to ask *do you need anything?* Mike shook his head imperceptibly and turned his attention back to Sierra.

"Do you need anything? Water?"

She shook her head. She was looking at him with a befuddled expression. It was probably the pregnancy.

Even though Mike hadn't been around a lot of pregnant women, he was learning fast.

Sierra became tearful at the drop of a hat. Her emotions were all over the place. But mostly she seemed having a strong reaction to him.

He looked into her bright green eyes. They had a watery quality that they hadn't had ten years ago.

It was the pregnancy. It had nothing to do with him no matter how much he imagined it. Or how much he wanted it to have something to do with him.

Perhaps he should be putting his energy toward trying to figure out *his* reaction to *her.*

He'd imagined seeing her again. Imagined what she might be like all grown up.

But he hadn't expected to have this kind of reaction.

He was reacting to the real person. The real Sierra. Not the Sierra he had carried in his head all these the years. The imaginary grown up version.

He reached out and put a hand over hers.

This Sierra was real.

And she might just be his undoing.

Wynter, dressed now in a sleek solid red dress now, came toward them with Bradford in tow.

She stood there, looking between him and her sister. Mike could see the questions she didn't ask.

But it was her wedding and Wynter would work this out in her head later.

Bradford, on the other hand, was so besotted with his new bride, he didn't seem to find it out of the ordinary in the least to see his best friend and his new sister-in-law sitting side by side. Again.

Mike moved his hand away from Sierra's.

"We're leaving now," Wynter said. "Will you be alright?"

Sierra looked at Mike, then back to her sister. A little smile played about her lips now. "I think I'm in good hands. "Mike is watching out for me." Sierra stood up and hugged her sister.

The statement caught Mike off guard.

Maybe he wasn't so far off base after all.

CHAPTER 22

*S*ierra was happy for her sister. But that didn't keep her from missing her the minute she and Bradford walked out the door.

They were only going on their honeymoon to Mackinac Island. They'd be back.

Besides, with Bradford being a pilot, they'd never be more than a short time away if she needed them.

She studied Mike under her lashes. Mike was a pilot, too. She wondered what it would be like to fly with him.

Perhaps she'd find out some day soon.

She was being fanciful again. But she found the baffled look on Mike's face endearing.

Mike was standing across the room now, near the door, talking to Noah and Savannah. She had a clear view of his profile.

He and Noah were about the same height and build. About six feet tall. Good sturdy build. Not too big, but not thin.

They were both handsome men with short dark hair. Noah was several years older, but they could be bothers.

Savannah glanced in her direction, saw her watching them, and smiled.

Sierra smiled back.

Just then Mike glanced in her direction. When his gaze met hers, she felt her cheeks flush. She was still smiling.

He waited a second, then his lips broke into a slow smile.

Sierra felt a flame of connection shoot between them. Everyone else – including Noah and Savannah – ceased to exist.

With that one look, she knew. She wasn't being fanciful.

There was an attraction between them.

Mike shook Noah's hand and hugged Savannah, then broke away and walked toward her.

Her heart rate went into overdrive.

Mike reached her side, held out his hand. "Want to get out of here?"

Sierra looked around. With Wynter and Bradford gone, there was really no one left that she wanted to visit with.

She suddenly realized that Mike was the reason she'd stayed so long. If he hadn't been here, she would have left when Wynter did.

She could be back in her hotel room now. Resting.

She put her hand in Mike's. Strong. Gentle. In that touch she felt possibilities.

And hope for the future.

A future she hadn't dared to dream of, much less think of as being possible.

CHAPTER 23

*M*ike wanted Sierra to be impressed. He wanted things to be perfect with her.

He led her through the pizzeria to the sound of Taylor Swift's *Begin Again.*

Apt, he thought. Although technically, they never began the first time. At least nowhere in the real world. Maybe in his head. A little.

Where did one take his pregnant girl after a wedding the day before Christmas Eve in the small town of Cassville at six o'clock in the evening?

Especially when said girl didn't know she was your girl?

They stepped outside into the glow of the moonlight. The weather was cold, but not unbearable.

He actually found it invigorating, but Sierra pulled her coat closer and shivered just a bit. They were dressed up for the wedding. Her in a red dress and him in a black tux. It seemed a shame to waste the opportunity.

Typically he would take a girl to dinner in this situation. But the pizzeria they'd just left was the best place on the island to eat.

Besides, they were dressed in their best. It seemed like for something better than pizza.

The sound of a plane that had just taken off from the local airport buzzed overhead. That would be Bradford and Wynter headed off to their honeymoon on Mackinac Island.

It occurred to Mike in that moment that he, too, was a pilot. With a plane.

They weren't limited to this small island where they'd all grown up.

He glanced over at Sierra and she smiled. His heart did a funny little summersault.

They may not have to be here, but at the moment, he was content.

He took her hand and laced his fingers lightly with hers. They walked down the sidewalk, past the hotel entrance, into the downtown area. All the stores were closed and they were the only ones on the street.

Both sides of Main Street were lit with small sparkly blue Christmas lights giving the air a crisp, cold glow beneath the moonlight.

A cat crossed the road ahead of them, nothing but a shadow in the cold light.

Sierra's hand tightened on his.

They walked slowly, not talking for several minutes.

"Do you ever miss not living here?" Her voice sounded a bit wistful. Like maybe she was missing living here right now.

He tried to think about living here. It had been so long ago. And he had been so very young.

His life was nothing like it had been when he'd been growing up here.

A picture of his life in Dallas/Fort Worth flashed through his mind. If he missed anything, it was the city.

He'd never been a small-town boy. "Not even a little." He looked at her. "Do you miss living here?"

She grinned. "Not even a little."

CHAPTER 24

It was just two days until Christmas Eve. A time when the city – any city - would be bustling with last-minute shopping.

But the sleepy little town of Cassville was already tucked in for the night.

Twinkly blue Christmas lights gave the town a cold, but Christmassy glow.

Sierra didn't miss Cassville. She'd never really fit in here and her memories of the town were conflicted.

But now, walking along Main Street with Mike, she missed what could have been.

Life could have been so different if she hadn't been troubled and he hadn't left here so long before she had.

Their paths had crossed only briefly back then, but the impact had been everlasting.

If her sister hadn't lost touch with Bradford…

So many ifs. So many lost possibilities.

But here they were now. Who would have thought her sister would accidentally get back with her high school sweetheart? Inadvertently putting Sierra and Mike back in each other's paths.

But all was not perfect. Sierra was expecting a child by another man. And Mike had absolutely no reason to be tangled up with her.

No man in his right mind would get involved with someone in her predicament.

They walked past the general store. They'd left their sound system with outside speakers on for the night.

Mariah Carey's "All I Want for Christmas" blasted over the night air.

Just for a moment, Sierra could indulge herself in the fantasy.

She was here. Walking down Main Street of her childhood town, hand-in-hand with Mike. The object of her teenage fantasies… her young adult fantasies…

Her current fantasies.

Mike had a place in her heart. She couldn't even remember a day when she didn't think about him at least once.

She hadn't obsessed over him and she'd obviously moved on, but still… he was an indelible part of her life.

And they hadn't even ever had a romantic involvement.

Mike slowed his pace and turned to her as the music faded into the background. "What do you want for Christmas, Sierra?"

Sierra nearly stumbled. Mike tightened his hold on her hand, keeping her steady.

She didn't answer.

But the answer flashed through her mind, clear as the crisp, clean winter air.

All she wanted for Christmas was him.

CHAPTER 25

The cold winter air carried the scent of impending snowfall. A clean scent. Clean and cold. Music from the general store had faded into the traditional, heart-wrenching *Oh Come All Ye Faithful.*

Sierra had a deer-in-the-headlights look on her face.

He'd asked what she wanted for Christmas to tease her, mostly.

But now he really, really wanted to know.

She was standing beneath a lantern shining clear white light over her face. The white light accentuated the blush on her cheeks.

A strand of hair had come loose and curved across her collarbone.

He'd never seen her look more beautiful.

He couldn't help himself. He reached out and stroked the soft skin of her cheek with a fingertip.

She blinked and her eyes closed. Her dark lashes smudged the skin beneath her eyes.

Mike swallowed, forcing his besotted brain to function.

"Sierra." He nudged her chin up with his fingertip.

Her eyes opened and he met her spellbinding green gaze. He could contentedly lose himself in those eyes.

"What do you want for Christmas? Really?" His voice sounded husky to his own ears.

"I… um…" She pulled away, turning her back to him.

Mike's heart sank.

He'd pushed too hard and overwhelmed her. He'd frightened her away.

He was still trying to figure out how to fix it when she answered.

"It's been so long since anyone asked me that." Her voice was so soft he had to strain to hear it. Then she lifted her chin and turned back to him. "I want to start my life over again. To reinvent myself."

Mike bit back his knee-jerk response. He didn't want her to change a thing. But he understood that need to do so.

He'd experienced something similar once just before he left Cassville. He'd felt that drive to start over. And he'd done it, too. He was no longer the boy who'd left here.

"How can I help?" he asked.

The question surprised her. She'd expected his first response then. She hadn't expected understanding and acceptance.

CHAPTER 26

Sierra fisted her hands in her coat pockets.

She was so cold, but her heart was melting with warmth on the inside.

It wasn't just the sparkly blue Christmas lights or the mournful music drifting from the general store. It wasn't just the clean scent of impending snow.

It was Mike. She'd always felt a kindred connection with him. He seemed to understand her like no one else did.

Still, she really didn't know that much about him. She knew he had a sister named Tiffany who lived somewhere in Europe, France maybe. He'd said he'd never been married, but she couldn't see a man as handsome and charming as he was not having girlfriends.

She knew he was a pilot and owned his own company. Did some contract work for Noah at Skye Travels.

That was it.

He was looking at her with his beautiful blue eyes. Eyes that had little creases around the outside corners. That locked onto hers like she was the most beautiful woman in the world.

His handsome features, the smile tugging at the corners of his mouth.

She also knew that he was kind. And giving. And a steadfast friend.

That was really all she needed to know.

"Come on," he said, taking her hand.

With him tugging her across the street, a bubble of laughter spilled from her lips. She put her free hand over her mouth, startled by the unexpected sound of her own laughter.

"Where are we going?" she asked as they stepped onto the curb on the other side of the street.

Even though she asked, it really didn't matter. Mike brought magic to her life and she'd go anywhere with him.

Turning, he looked at her, grinning sheepishly. "We're all dressed up, so... I think we should go somewhere fitting."

She smiled. She couldn't help it. It was like a bubble of happiness had exploded on top of her head.

Sierra felt light as she walked beside him, hand in hand. Lighter than she'd felt in so very long.

It didn't matter at the moment that she'd vowed to keep to herself. To focus on her baby. To reinvent her life.

It wouldn't hurt to spend the evening with Mike.

Just once.

CHAPTER 27

$\mathcal{M}$ ike mapped out his flight path, sent it in, and within minutes they were cleared for take-off. The roar of the plane's motor was all he could hear, but to him, it was as beautiful as a cat's purr.

Sierra sat in the passenger seat of his little Cessna Mustang - his favorite airplane. He'd had the seats redone in a buttery soft charcoal gray leather.

The charcoal gray was a perfect backdrop for Sierra's Christmas red dress.

She wore the headphones without seeming to even notice that they messed up her hair.

He rarely had anyone up front with him. Passengers almost always sat in the back. He supposed it was a lot like being a taxi driver. He was the pilot and the flight attendant. And sometimes even the mechanic.

In an unfortunate way, he had been fortunate. His uncle had died just as Mike was entering college. Uncle Daniel had never married and never had children. Having no heirs, he'd left Mike and his sister a windfall of money.

Mike never talked about this. Other than Bradford, he

hadn't told anyone. Everyone just thought he'd been amazingly successful.

He had been, but only because he'd caught a booster at a very young age. Brilliant business man? Not so much. At least nothing like his friend Noah Worthington.

Mike had watched from the sidelines as Noah had built his empire. Mike was ready to jump in if his friend needed any help, but Noah had done it all by himself.

"Ready?" He grinned at Sierra.

She looked up at him and smiled. She shrugged sweetly.

Mike navigated the plane onto the runway and prepared for take-off.

In just two hours, maybe a little less, they would land in New York. He'd gone with his first impulse. New York was his favorite city.

Perhaps Sierra would like it, too.

CHAPTER 28

S ierra squeezed a fist, digging her nails into the palm of her hand.

She was not, it seemed, dreaming.

Mike hadn't told her where they were going. He said he wanted it to be a surprise.

Sierra recognized the New York City skyline as soon as the endless bright lights unfolded on the ground beneath them.

She kept her face turned toward the window so Mike couldn't see the tears that welled up in her eyes.

It had to be the stupid hormones. It couldn't possibly be that the guy who brought magic to her life had taken her to a magical place.

Sierra had always wanted to visit New York. The quintessential hub of art and music.

They'd brought their luggage and Sierra honestly thought he was taking her back to Madison.

About a hundred different thoughts were running through her head. What were they going to do here in New

York? Were they spending the night? If so, where would they stay? For how long?

Using a skill she'd learned long ago, she shoved all the thoughts aside. All the possibilities. And forced herself not to get carried away. She pushed away the child-like excitement that was bubbling up inside her.

The reality was this was a one-time thing.

Mike doubtlessly had some free time and he didn't have anything else to do for the evening. He'd probably avoided scheduling anything other than the wedding for the evening.

But we brought our luggage.

Sierra hadn't flown much, but she knew a smooth landing when she saw it. It took several minutes to taxi to the private jet area.

Other than what sounded like a few mumbles into his microphone, Mike sat in silence. The silence was companionable and surprisingly not awkward at all. Somehow she'd thought of Mike as being more verbose.

She hadn't expected to feel so comfortable with him. When she was a teen, he'd seemed much more intense.

Catching her studying him, Mike grinned at her. "How about dinner?"

She grinned back. Not that she could have helped responding to his charm even if she'd been inclined to do so.

Then she shrugged. "Sure. Why not?"

She was determined to enjoy the evening.

Even if it was just one night.

CHAPTER 29

*M*ike had reserved a rental car and it was waiting at the gate for them.

"Mr. Phillips." The young valet, not a day over twenty, shook Mike's hand. "I hope this 535 is ok with you."

Mike looked at the shiny white BMW 535 sedan. "It's perfect, Garth."

"Yes sir. I know you usually reserve an M5." Garth acknowledged Sierra, then turned his gaze back to Mike. "But at the last minute, there wasn't one available."

"No worries, Garth." Mike clapped the younger man on the shoulder and took the key fob. "It's more than I expected, to be honest."

Garth beamed and opened the passenger door.

"I've got this. Thank you." Mike held out his hand for Sierra.

There were benefits to being a regular. He had a client, a prolific author, who visited New York once a month. As a result, Mike had not only become astoundingly familiar with the city, but several people, including the airport staff, had become very familiar with him.

Who would have thought a small-town boy from Cassville, Wisconsin would have grown up to be perceived as a New Yorker?

But tonight was different. Tonight he was seeing what had become routine through the eyes of someone he wanted to share it with. Someone he cared about.

Garth brought their luggage from the plane and put it in the trunk while Mike settled Sierra in the passenger seat.

With one arm on the open door, he stood a moment and looked at Sierra. Just looked at her.

She looked good sitting on the soft black leather seats. She smiled at him, lifted one delicate eyebrow, her lips curving in a questioning smile.

Yes, Mike decided.

Sierra looked good in his life.

He went around to the driver's seat and was happy to see that the GPS was already set to the hotel.

Most people would have taken a taxi into the city from the airport, but Mike liked to have his own car available. He should probably reconsider that habit, though, since he usually just parked it at the hotel and walked or took public transportation from there.

Ah well. You could take the boy out of the small town, but you couldn't expect to take all the small town from the boy.

He shrugged and put the car into drive.

He needed to stay focused. Driving in New York required more concentration than flying into the city.

It was especially difficult with the lovely Sierra Jordan in his passenger seat.

CHAPTER 30

*S*ierra straightened the white cloth napkin in her lap and stared into the flickering flames of the candle in the middle of the table. A matching white tablecloth covered the table.

The elegant restaurant was somewhere in Manhattan overlooking Central Park. Soft classical music played in the background, masking the traffic sounds on the street outside. The energy in the city was even more than Sierra had expected, much less imagined.

She sat in a soft booth across from Mike.

The server wearing a black tuxedo came to their table and offered wine or cocktails.

Mike declined without a hitch.

Sierra's heart warmed. Mike had obviously not only remembered her pregnancy, but also adapted his drink of choice to water.

After the server left, Mike set aside his menu and leaned forward. "Have you thought about baby names?"

Sierra's breath hitched. They hadn't talked about her

pregnancy. And somehow she'd thought she could avoid it. It was silly, really.

A pregnancy wasn't something anyone could just ignore. Not for any length of time anyway.

She met his gaze and took a deep, steadying breath. "I haven't thought about names yet. Not much anyway."

"Huh." He sat back.

"Huh what?" She sat up straighter, leaned back a bit, too.

"Nothing." He shook his head. "I just had the idea that mothers always knew what they were going to name their children long before they even got pregnant."

Sierra shrugged and looked across the restaurant. It was late, but all the tables were still filled.

Conversation and laughter swirled around them. New Yorkers having a normal evening out. Even Mike, a man who'd grown up in a small town, seemed at home here.

Sierra was envious. She was a small-town girl who longed for more. She'd moved to Madison, but Madison didn't require a significant amount of lifestyle changes.

But New York... New York was a different world entirely.

She looked back at Mike. She loved how he looked boyish when he was unsure of himself. Like now.

"You know," she said. "I didn't exactly plan this."

"Still..." He leaned forward. Ran a fingertip along the edge of his water glass.

Sierra shook her head. "Not even a little."

He sipped his water and watched her in silence.

She straightened. "I think it might actually be a good thing, though."

"The pregnancy? In what way?"

She took a deep, ragged breathe. Her gaze darted around the room, then back to his spellbinding blue eyes.

Sierra hadn't told anyone about the impact the pregnancy

was having on her. On her life. Her goals. Her outlook on life.

She'd kept her thoughts closely guarded.

If anyone else knew, they might criticize her. To call her selfish.

She was afraid that if anyone else knew, her resolve would crumble and she would collapse back into the person she was before.

But this was Mike. The keeper of her secrets.

Perhaps she could tell him. A little, at least. "It's prompted me to change the way I look at life."

He nodded. "I can only imagine. Anything specific?"

She swallowed and felt the tears welling in her eyes. Stupid hormones. She blinked and looked away. She clasped her hands together on the table and squeezed them tightly.

He reached out and put a hand over hers. "It's ok. You can tell me later."

She closed her eyes and felt a tear slide down her cheek.

She pulled a hand away from his and swiped it the tear. "I'm sorry," she whispered.

"Sierra," he said.

She didn't answer. She couldn't. And she couldn't look at him right now. She fought the lump in her throat.

But this time, she didn't run away.

CHAPTER 31

Mike got up and slid into the booth beside Sierra.

"Hey," he murmured. He'd never been bothered much by a woman's tears. But this was different. This was Sierra.

And her tears were breaking his heart.

He pulled her close, cupping the back of her head. He could feel her warm breath through the cotton fabric of his white shirt. Her hair was incredibly soft and smelled like lavender.

"It's ok," he murmured.

The server came to their table, set down their water glasses, and silently walked away.

He'd never known anyone who fought tears as hard as Sierra did.

He ran a hand gently over her back, over the smooth taffeta.

Her warm tears soaked his shirt as she silently cried. Then she took a deep breath and blew it out slowly.

She pulled back, keeping her gaze down. "I must look like a raccoon." She used the cloth napkin to dap at her eyes.

"I like raccoons."

She laughed just a little. But it was enough to stop the last of her tears. "I'm so sorry." She wiped at his damp shirt.

"You have nothing to apologize for." He wanted to hold her again and never let her go.

"I should go to the restroom to make sure I don't scare anyone."

"Sure. But you look fine to me," he said, standing up and holding out his hand. "I'll walk with you."

She took his hand and slid over, stood up. "Ok, but I promise I won't run away this time."

"Especially here in New York." He held out his hand. "Pinky promise?"

Laughing, she linked her pinky with his. "Yes. Pinky promise." Blinking, looked up at him. "But I have to tell you something."

"You can tell me anything."

"I'm not fifteen anymore."

Minutes later, Mike stood outside the restroom door, waiting for Sierra.

She seemed to think he hadn't noticed that she was no longer a teenager.

He hardly even thought of her that way at all. His thoughts had put the two versions of her together into a nice package. Combining the old with the new.

But definitely adult.

He would have to figure out a way to assure her that he no longer thought of her as a kid.

CHAPTER 32

Sierra stood at the sink in the restroom and repaired her make-up.

Thank God for waterproof mascara. She had no more than a few smudges of black on her cheeks and, thankfully, hadn't ruined Mike's white shirt.

She would have been mortified.

It was bad enough to break into a crying fit right there in front of him. In his arms, no less.

All he'd done was listen to her. And ask about how her pregnancy had changed the way she looked at life.

It wasn't that big a deal.

Except that no one else had asked her those questions.

Or even listened to her enough to realize that the pregnancy *had* changed the way she looked at life.

Now she had to go back out there and face him.

The one person that she cared enough to worry about how he saw her. To want him to see her as being put together and not falling apart.

She swiped some lip gloss over her lips and squared her shoulders.

She still didn't know what he had planned for them.

They'd dropped their luggage off at the hotel. Along with the car.

Then they'd taken a taxi to the restaurant. It was all very unusual.

But then Sierra didn't know much about life in the big city.

Perhaps one day she would be as comfortable as Mike was here.

But then he was comfortable in any situation.

She opened the door to the ladies' lounge and stepped out.

Mike was leaning against the wall on the opposite side of the hallway. Close enough that he could see the door, but not so close as to make other women uncomfortable.

He was socially skilled in such things.

He saw her and grinned.

Her heart did a funny little flip flop.

Oh my, but he was a handsome man. Even here in a city of handsome man, there was none more handsome than he was.

When she stopped in front of him, he pulled a rose from behind his back and handed it to her.

She took the lovely red bud with moisture clinging to it, closed her eyes, and sniffed it.

It smelled as beautiful as it looked. "Where did you get this?" She looked around, but saw no vendors. No one else with flowers.

"It's New York," he said. "Anything is possible."

CHAPTER 33

Almost Midnight

New York. A city where anything is possible.

Mike held open the door and followed Sierra out onto the 102nd floor of the Empire State Building.

It was late and there were only a few other people around. One of them was a young man with a camera. There were two other couples, one dressed casually and the other in formal attire.

It was the first time Mike had been up the Empire State Building since they'd glassed in the top floor. The last time he'd been up, the top floor with the unparalleled views had been windy and cold. His date, he used the word date loosely, had been miserable.

Oddly enough, he couldn't even remember the young lady's name. All he remembered was that she was the daughter of a one one-time client.

Mike rarely bothered with one-time clients. He stayed busy enough with his regulars. He'd been free that particular week and, well, the destination was New York. What he did remember most was the burden of what he came to think of as babysitting.

Even if the *baby* was in her twenties.

That was water under the bridge now, though.

Sierra's face lit up as she walked over to the floor-to-ceiling windows to look out over the city.

She put both gloved hands against the glass and looked down with obvious awe.

"Wow." Her voice was hushed. "It's beautiful."

"And that's not even the best part." He pointed toward the sky off to their right.

A bright full moon, in shades of silver and gray, hung just among the tops of the skyscrapers. As a pilot, Mike had seen a lot of full moons, but this was one of the clearest and biggest he'd seen in recent memory.

He stood behind Sierra, looking over her shoulder, resting one hand lightly at the waist of her wool coat.

She turned her head and lifted her gaze to his. "This is amazing."

"I've never seen it quite like this." He knew that the main reason he'd never seen it quite like this was because he'd never seen it through Sierra's eyes. With her standing with him.

She turned around the rest of the way, putting her all but in his arms. Her cheeks were flushed, her eyes sparkling in the moonlight.

He gave up, groaned, and pulled her to him in a hug, wrapping his arms around her.

His fingers threaded in her long, soft hair and he kissed the top of her head.

She relaxed against him. They just stood that way, the seconds slipping past.

Neither one of them moved.

Then, seemingly at the same time, they pulled back a

little.

His gaze locked onto hers.

He realized in that moment that there was no one else he wanted to be with.

Her lips were parted a little, as though she might be thinking the same thing.

It was enough.

He lowered his head and pressed his lips against hers.

CHAPTER 34

Sierra dug her fingers into Mike's coat.

His lips, soft and firm, pressed lightly against hers.

Every dream, every fantasy she'd had since she was a teen-age girl coalesced with reality.

The deep motor of a jet flying overhead. The sounds of footsteps as people walked around the observatory. Back and forth toward the elevators.

The dry cleaner smell of Mike's wool coat. A hint of his masculine soap still lingering on his skin.

All these things reminded her that this moment in time was real and not imagined like so many other moments with him that had only existed in her head.

She felt the kiss from her lips all the way to her toes.

She was dizzy from the height of the Empire State Building. From standing next to Mike.

From the feel of his lips on hers.

She was afraid to open her eyes.

Afraid if she did, she'd be dreaming again.

This was Mike.

Her one true love.
And just once she hoped it was for real.
He shifted and pulled his lips from hers.
Feeling the loss, she swayed and opened her eyes.
He was smiling at her.
She smiled back.
And promptly fainted.

CHAPTER 35

The earth spun off its axis as Mike caught Sierra just as she fainted in his arms.

Everything around him ceased to exist. All he could see was her beautiful face, pale, her lips parted, her eyes rolling back.

Normal conversations swirled around him as he lowered her to the ground.

No one seemed to notice that the love of his life was unconscious.

The faint sound of a siren drifted from the streets below.

Helpless fear rose in the back of his throat.

His past flashed before him.

He'd waited too long. Now he would never get the chance to tell her that he was in love with her and had been since she was a teenager.

Kneeling beside her, he put his fingertips against her neck. Reminded himself that he was trained in first aid. He had to be. As a pilot, he was entrusted with people's lives and he was the one passengers would look to in a time of crisis.

He'd never had to use his first aid training until now.

All those years and now it was Sierra needing his help.

He couldn't make sense of it.

Someone, finally, apparently noticed that she was unconscious. "Is she ok?" the man asked over his shoulder.

He refrained from shouting the words that came to mind. *Does she look alright to you?* Instead, he answered calmly. "No." He looked the young man in the eye and ignored the rush of empathy that he felt for the poor guy right behind the anger. "Call 911."

The young man nodded and raced off.

Mike took a deep breath. She'd fainted, that was all.

But why? Something was wrong for this happen. It may very well have something to do with her pregnancy.

Mike sat back on his heels. He was no doctor. But this was not right.

Maybe he'd kept her out too late. They'd had dinner, so it wasn't from hunger.

Maybe it was from the stress of the day. Her sister had gotten married, then he'd taken her flying to New York.

Perhaps it was too much for a normal person, much less a pregnant one.

He ran a hand through his hair.

He was going to make himself crazy.

He glanced around. The guy was watching him out of the corner of his eye, a cell phone pressed to his ear.

Turning back to Sierra, he gently patted her cheek. Her skin was cool.

But her eyes fluttered open. "Mike." She breathed his name, then closed her eyes again.

There was a little more color to her cheeks now. Either that or he was imagining it.

Willing her to wake up, he took off his coat and put it under her head. He hated having her lying here on the gritty floor.

He pressed his fingertips against his eyes. He needed to think.

He stood up, bent over, and, putting one arm under her knees and the other behind her shoulders, picked up her. Cradling her close to him, he walked to a bench and sat down with her in his arms.

Sitting there on the little bench at the top of the Empire State Building, his thoughts shot back to a day over ten years ago.

Sierra had been taken to a detention center at Cassville. It wasn't there anymore. Now all the arrests are taken to Dubuque.

She'd called him. Out of all the people in the world that she could have called – her sister Wynter, her parents, even Bradford.

She'd called him.

Can you come get me? She'd asked, her voice soft. Even now he remembered hearing the unexpected vein of fear in her voice.

Of course. He remembered thinking that she was probably at a school dance or some such. Maybe her date had left her. *Where are you?*

Even over the phone line, he'd heard her swallow. Almost heard her close her eyes. "I'm in the detention center."

He hadn't believed her. There had to be a mistake.

He remembered feeling grateful that he was in town at the time. Even though he'd been in town, he was certain he would have dropped what he'd been doing – from wherever he'd been flying – and found his way to the Cassville Detention Center.

But more than anything, he remembered the look on her face when they led her out of the room.

Though she held her chin high, her face had been

streaked with tears. And he'd seen her bottom lip tremble just before he'd pulled her into a hug.

He hadn't commented when he'd heard the little sniffle she tried valiantly to hide.

They gave her purse back to her. Her phone. And she'd grabbed onto them like a lifeline.

He'd kept his arm around her as they left the center.

"They're on their way," the young man told him, jarring him back the present.

"Thank you," Mike said to the young man, but kept his gaze on Sierra.

He'd wanted her in his arms, but not like this.

His lips still tingled from the feel of the kiss.

So many emotions swirled through him. Fear. Concern. Hopefulness.

Love.

CHAPTER 36

Sierra woke slowly. Her first impression was a vague sense that she was not in her own bed.

There were strange smells. Sterile. Antiseptic, perhaps.

And strange sounds. There was an echo in the room. An echo, but there were background noises. Sierra's apartment was quiet. She often forgot she even had neighbors. Besides, this sounded more like someone in her apartment.

Strangers.

She opened her eyes and confirmed what she already knew. She was not at home. There was a television right in front of her.

Sierra didn't have a television in her bedroom.

A slight movement of her hand and she knew. She was in the hospital.

There was an IV in the back of her hand and electrodes on her chest.

A hand slid automatically to the little baby bump.

She blew out a breath. It was still there.

The baby bump was the first thing she felt in the morning and the last thing she felt at night.

She tried to wrap her brain around why she was here in the hospital.

She closed her eyes and allowed her thoughts to settle.

Mike.

She'd been with Mike.

There had been a kiss.

She brought her left hand to her lips and played the moment back over in her mind.

She'd fainted.

She had a vague memory of being in Mike's arms.

Opening her eyes, she looked around. New York. They were in New York.

But where was Mike? She rested her hands on her abdomen again.

He'd left her here.

Alone.

A nurse walked into the room. "Well, good morning." The nurse smiled cheerfully. "You're awake."

"What happened?" Sierra asked.

The nurse checked her vitals. "The doctor will be in to talk with you before long. But you're gonna be just fine."

Sierra didn't answer. She may be *just fine* physically, but her heart wasn't just fine.

She didn't know what she was going to be without Mike.

Sierra's thoughts wandered while the nurse chatted.

He'd kissed her, then he'd left her.

He'd come to his senses, that was all. She was too young. She was pregnant.

Then the nurse said something that got her attention. "I'm sorry. What did you say?"

"I said that young man of yours has been beside himself waiting for you to wake up." She reached the door and added over her shoulder. "I'll let him know you're awake so he can come see you."

Sierra's heart soared. He was here. And he wanted to see her.

That young man of yours.

She relaxed against the pillows for a moment, letting herself imagine.

Imagine a life where Mike was her man.

When she opened her eyes again, he was standing in the doorway grinning at her.

CHAPTER 37

Christmas music drifted softly from the cracked hospital door leading to the hallway. Besides the antiseptic scent of the hospital, he could smell the cheerful yellow daffodils on the window sill behind him.

He'd considered sending roses, but chose daffodils for their strong cheerful scent. He could sent her roses later.

Mike was a besotted fool.

And he was loving it.

He'd always wondered what it must feel like to be totally and completely head over heels in love with someone.

Sure. He'd had crushes. And he'd even imagined himself in love a few times. He was well acquainted with that particular giddy feeling.

But this particular feeling of caring more about this other person than anything else was new to him.

He'd already cancelled the flight he had in two days.

He'd never cancelled a flight for anyone. Of course, he'd had no reason to, but he wasn't sure he would have.

Especially not after just a simple kiss.

But this was Sierra.

She was that special person that took precedence over everything else.

Now he just had to figure out what to do about all of this.

Sierra's cheeks were flushed.

"What did the doctor say?" she asked.

The doctor. Right. "You just got a little light-headed and fainted. That's all. Nothing to worry about."

"Nothing to worry about." She lifted her hand where the IV was stuck under her skin. "Doesn't feel like nothing."

Mike laughed, relief flooding through him. He sat down in the chair next to her and threaded his fingers through hers.

He locked his gaze onto hers. "Sierra." He was unprepared for the lump in his throat. He swallowed thickly.

Her eyes misty, she blinked and a single tear slipped down her cheek.

"Sierra." Mike's heart was swollen bigger than any Grinch and he thought it might explode.

He wanted to pull her close and hug her, but she had too many wires attached.

There would be another time.

"What is it?" she asked, her voice coming out in no more than a whisper. She moved her hand over her abdomen. "The baby?"

"No," he quickly shook his head. He needed to just spit it out. He was torturing her. The last person he wanted to torture.

"I love you," he said.

CHAPTER 38

Sierra closed her eyes and gripped the cool sheet. It felt real enough. But one thought kept circling through her mind.

She'd died and gone to Heaven.

"I've always loved you," Mike said, his voice full of... happiness.

Could this be real? She opened her eyes and searched his face. She took a deep steadying breath.

It was real.

"Love you, too." The words came automatic, putting a voice to the feelings that she'd been dancing around.

His face broke into a grin. "You do?"

She nodded.

Then he was out of his chair. And his lips were pressed gently against hers.

It was a moment of bliss.

Before she remembered.

She was a package deal.

She had to think about her child.

Shaking her head, she felt her heart break just a little. "I can't."

Mike sat back in his chair. He was a smart man. Probably the smartest man Sierra knew. "I'm not afraid of the baby," he said.

"It's too much," she said, ignoring the surprise at this statement and the little bit of hope that went along with it. "It's not yours."

"Well, it's yours, isn't it?"

She looked at him blankly a moment, then laughed. "As far as we know."

"We're good then," he said. "If you find out it's not yours, we might have a problem."

"You'll be the first to know." She held onto his hand like a lifeline.

They were still staring into each other's eyes when the nurse popped into the room.

"Guess what?" the nurse said. "You can go home."

Sierra knew she was in trouble, when her first thought was *no*. She didn't want to go home because it meant she had to let go of Mike's hand.

CHAPTER 39

Mike had reserved two rooms at the hotel.

But after he got Sierra settled into her bed, he couldn't bring himself to leave.

It wasn't just that she might need something. He was pretty sure that she would actually be ok. It was more that he didn't want to be away from her.

He lay on the sofa of the one room suite. It was plush enough as far as hotel rooms went. He'd stayed in nicer and he'd stayed in worse.

This was one of his favorites. It had everything he needed. A Starbuck's in the lobby. A dry-cleaning service to the room. A work out room. And it was in the perfect location for some of his favorite restaurants in Manhattan.

He'd noticed, earlier while he was out getting a coffee, that there was a day care. It was funny how he'd never noticed it before. He was so surprised, in fact, that he'd stopped and asked one of the workers if they were new.

She said she'd worked there for five years. Yes, in that location.

Mike was just astounded that he'd been coming to this

hotel and he'd never noticed that there was a day care on the first floor.

He'd been so ensconced in his own childfree world. How many other things had he missed?

He hadn't given much thought to children. It was something other people did. And *maybe* something for him one day.

It didn't bother him that he wasn't the father. Not even a little bit. Mike was adopted. And he had a soft spot for children who had no family

But this child had family. This child had a mother. A mother Mike was besotted with.

He lifted his phone to check the time.

It was just after noon.

But more importantly, it was Christmas Eve.

Christmas Eve in New York.

Christmas Eve with Sierra.

He sat up and looked across the room at Sierra. She was still asleep.

He wanted to make this Christmas Eve special for her.

He had time to plan something, but he had to make it something special.

But what would be special enough to be worthy of his first Christmas with Sierra?

CHAPTER 40

Sierra had really slept in.

Last night had been so surreal. It had started with her sister getting married in Cassville, Wisconsin and ended up with her spending the night in the hospital in New York.

Yesterday morning, she never could have predicted that today she would be waking up in a hotel room in New York.

Mike had been here earlier, but he wasn't here now. She knew that without even opening her eyes.

She could sense that he wasn't there. Besides, she'd heard the door close behind him a about two, maybe three hours ago, just as she was pulling herself out a deep sleep.

After he left, she'd decided to go back to sleep. Just for a little while.

Now she'd had so much sleep, she felt a bit groggy.

She sat up and put her feet on the soft carpeted floor.

This was one time she was tempted to break her own rule and have a cup of coffee.

If not for the baby, she'd probably do it.

But, she reminded herself, the baby was the most important thing right now.

And for the next rest of her life.

She stood up and stretched.

It felt so good to get up and move around.

She twirled her arms and that's when she saw the note on the other pillow.

She leaned across the bed and picked up the note written on hotel stationary.

Dear Sierra,

Merry Christmas Eve!

I have a surprise planned for you.

I'm giving you some privacy to get ready.

Please meet me in the lobby at six o'clock.

Love,

Mike

Sierra stared at those two words, savoring them. Like a sip of fine wine. Letting them sink into her mind.

Love Mike.

Then after seconds, maybe minutes had passed, she went back and reread the rest of the note again.

So formal.

She'd never actually seen his handwriting.

Besides being so formal, he had a lovely handwriting.

She held the note to her chest and sighed. There was nothing about Mike that she didn't like.

Except maybe… that he may very well be playing with her heart.

She had an impression of him, right or wrong, that he could love a girl, then leave her without a qualm.

She sincerely hoped she was wrong about that.

And in that spirit, she'd decided to give him a chance.

It was Mike. And if anyone deserved the chance to prove her wrong, he did.

So he had something planned for their Christmas Eve in New York.

She didn't even know how long he'd initially intended for them to stay. Or even if he had other plans for Christmas.

She didn't have any plans. Except for a quiet day spent at her apartment working on some future plans.

Nonetheless, her first order of business was to take a bath.

She went into the bathroom to run her bathwater and that's when she saw the dress.

Hanging from the shower curtain was one of the most beautiful dresses she'd ever seen.

It was a floor length maroon gown with an empire waist and a full skirt. The long sleeves were sheer and the neckline was high.

But the most interesting thing about the dress was the way it shimmered with what looked like a thousand lightening bugs.

Wow. She was supposed to wear this then.

Mike never ceased to amaze her.

And then were gorgeous low heels in a matching maroon color.

She turned on the bath water and added some of her lavender bath soap.

Tonight was going to be interesting, to say the least.

CHAPTER 41

$\mathcal{M}$ike sat at the hotel bar, holding an untouched whiskey in his hands.

He wore a black tuxedo with a tie that matched the dress he'd gotten for Sierra.

He so hoped he'd gotten her size right. He didn't want her to be embarrassed by trying to wear a dress that was too small or too large.

Christmas music played in the background of the noisy bar. Meeting here was apparently a popular thing to do here on Christmas Eve.

Back in Cassville or most anywhere else in the country, for that matter, most people would be at home with their families.

Sharing gifts. Making deserts. Decorating trees.

Whatever family tradition they held dear.

But here in New York there were a lot of people without families. Like him. Or people who couldn't or chose not to be with their family. Like Sierra.

Sierra would be missing Wynter about now.

Mike was a little surprised that Sierra's sister had planned a Christmas honeymoon. She probably hadn't given it much thought that she'd be leaving her sister behind to spend time alone.

But Mike to the rescue.

It seemed to be what he did best when it came to Sierra.

He only hoped that she saw him as more than just a rescuer.

Tonight he would find out.

He'd planned out a date that would leave no doubt that he saw her as someone he wanted to spend time with.

He kept his eyes on the door. He was actually feeling nervous about seeing her.

There was always the possibility that she wouldn't come.

She could over sleep. The dress might not fit.

She might just decide she didn't want to see him.

He'd jumped off the edge when he'd signed the note *love Mike.*

He wanted to make sure that she knew his intentions were more than just friends.

Not that it mattered.

She saw him as the kind of man who threw the words around, not meaning them.

Sometimes he wished that was who he really was. It was easier to pretend to be that way than to actually be that way.

He looked down at his drink.

As a pilot, he'd left countless drinks untouched for a variety of reasons.

Sometimes he was entertaining, but had an upcoming flight.

Sometimes he just didn't feel like drinking, but didn't want to explain himself.

Sort of like tonight, but not exactly.

He'd had every intention of drinking the whiskey when he'd ordered it.

But he wanted to be clear-headed when he saw Sierra.

Besides, his innate sense of fairness wouldn't allow it. She couldn't drink, so it didn't seem right that he should get to.

Well-dressed beautiful women and men swirled around him. Most of them talking and laughing.

He realized belatedly, that he must appear morose in comparison.

But he wanted to give Sierra the chance to make her own choice about tonight.

He'd rather pulled her along, not really asking her what her preference was.

If he showed up at her hotel room door, she, again, would feel she had little choice but to go along with him.

But not this time.

He tapped his glass with his fingertips.

Laughed at himself.

He had everything planned out down to the dress that she would wear.

He would have to work on giving her more choices.

In fact, he decided right then and there that he'd take her shopping the day after Christmas and let her pick out something herself to wear.

If she wanted to.

He was hopeless.

He wouldn't have recognized her if not for the dress.

But the burgundy sparkly dress was one of a kind.

Its sparkles reminded him of lightening bugs. It had seemed perfect for her.

And it still did.

The dress sparkled even more beautiful with her in it.

She wore her hair down, the way he liked it best.

At first she didn't see him.

She looked a little lost. A little uncertain.

But absolutely beautiful.

Without taking his eyes off of her, he stood up.

That's when she recognized him. Her face lit up.

She floated toward him – the only way to describe the way she moved in that dress.

When she stood in front of him, she twirled around once. Looking over her shoulder she asked. "What do you think?"

He was too choked up to answer.

Little Sierra Jordan was the most beautiful women he'd ever seen.

And she was here. To spend the evening with him.

CHAPTER 42

Sierra's nerves were on edge. But she was determined to smile and have a good time.

As she'd soaked in the warm bath water, she'd considered that this might be her one chance to spend a fairy tale evening with Mike. And Christmas Eve at that.

She was the luckiest woman alive tonight.

Out of all the possible women, he'd chosen to spend his Christmas Eve with her.

She knew that some women would probably be offended that he'd picked out her dress and planned the evening without the least little bit of input from her.

She didn't care.

She thought it was charming.

And romantic.

It wasn't like she'd felt all that well lately. If he continued to plan things for her, she'd worry about it then.

But for right now, she was just going to enjoy the adventure.

And an adventure it was.

The worse part for her had been finding her way to the bar without him. Though she loved New York, she was a little intimidated by being here alone.

Nonetheless, she'd gotten lots of appreciative looks from both men and women.

It was the dress. She didn't look pregnant in it. Instead she felt like a princess.

And she was determined to enjoy it.

If only for just one night.

She spotted Mike across the crowded bar. When he stood up and smiled at her, all the other people in the room faded away.

"The dress is even more beautiful with you in it," he said. "More than I thought possible."

"So is that what you do? Buy a girl a pretty dress and charm her with fancy words?" She sat when he pulled out a chair for her.

"That depends." He sat next to her. Not across from her. "Are you charmed?"

Yes. "Well…" She straightened the skirts of the full gown. "It is a most beautiful dress." She looked at him, a mischievous look on her face. "A perfect fit."

"Nice." He looked at her sideways. "And no, I have not had a lot of practice in buying dresses for pretty girls."

She lifted an eyebrow.

"Or any girls," he continued. "or women."

"In that case, you may well be a natural."

He laughed. "It's always good to have a backup plan." He sobered. "How do you feel?"

"Rested." The server brought two glasses of water. "I wouldn't mind having some more of whatever they gave me in the hospital."

"Perhaps that can be arranged." He slid her water closer her way.

Sierra shrugged. "I doubt it. They're funny about the whole pregnancy thing."

"Rightly so." Mike leaned back in his chair and drank half his glass of water.

She watched him closely, though she wasn't sure what she was looking for. Some reluctance about the baby probably. Between Mike and the baby, she barely thought about anything else.

The problem was trying to put the two together. It was a bit like trying to put the proverbial square peg in a round hole.

The two just didn't seem to go together, no matter how hard she tried to fit them together in her head.

"I know an Italian place," he said, picking up a breadstick. "We have reservations in an hour."

"How did you manage reservations on Christmas Eve?"

He grinned. "I know a few people."

Sierra contemplated the idea of a boy from Cassville getting to know people in New York well enough to pull enough strings to get a reservation for dinner on Christmas Eve.

Her silence seemed to make him uncomfortable. "I hope you don't mind me making the plans. If you have something you'd rather do, we can readjust."

"Seriously? Besides the fact that I've never even been to New York, I just got out of the hospital. Not that there's anything wrong." She stopped, realizing that she was talking too much and bit her lip.

"Nothing wrong, huh?" His voice held more than a hint of sarcasm. "People just faint for no reason all the time."

"They didn't find anything wrong."

Mike shook his head. "All the same, your job is to take it easy and enjoy yourself."

"We'll see what happens," she said.

But she didn't tell him that she was already enjoying herself immensely.

CHAPTER 43

After dinner at a quaint little Italian restaurant, they stepped out onto the crowded sidewalk of Times Square. The air was festive. Christmas carols drifted from speakers overhead and videos flashed overhead.

New York on Christmas Eve. Nothing else like it. The scent of hot dogs drifted from a street vendor mixed with the scent of crisp cold air.

People bustled past, arms full of holiday shopping bags.

Mike clasped Sierra's hand. The last thing he needed was to lose her in this crowd.

"Wow," she said. "I've never seen anything quite like this before."

"There is nothing quite like it." He steered them past a street vendor.

"You never said what we're doing tonight."

"It's a surprise."

A man selling a bucket of flowers stepped up to Mike.

"How about a rose for a beautiful flower?" the man asked.

Mike was usually good at ignoring street vendors. This

man was unusually bold to stop someone who hadn't made eye contact.

He looked over at Sierra. Her eyes were bright and her cheeks were flushed. He wanted to keep her happy. Whatever it took.

He took a bill from his pocket, handed it to the seller, and took a dewy red rose bud from the man's bucket.

He handed it to Sierra. She closed her eyes, pressed the flower against her lips and inhaled deeply. When she opened her eyes, he saw an intensity of affectionate emotion that he wasn't prepared for.

His voice catching, he took her elbow. "Come on, my love, let's not be late."

He led her through the crowd toward Lincoln Center. It took them a little over thirty minutes, but they took their time. It was more of a stroll really.

Mike was content. This was already the best Christmas Eve he'd ever had.

As they approached the Lincoln Center, he immediately wished he'd hired a limo to drive them to the door.

The water fountain was aglow with white light and the tall Christmas tree was decorated with large white lights in the shape of snowflakes.

As they walked closer, all the lights blinked and became pink. Then silver. Then back to white.

They watched the light show as they stood in line to go inside. "What is this, she asked."

"Lincoln Center." He tried to keep his face straight.

She looked at him in confusion. "Lincoln Center..." Then her face lit up in a huge grin. "The New York Philharmonic?"

"Merry Christmas," he said, bending down to kiss her on the forehead.

The look on her face was everything and more than he ever could have asked for.

He had no way of knowing how she felt about classical music.

While they stood in line, a light snowfall started. He watched as the light snowflakes landed in Sierra's hair. On her coat.

It struck him that he'd never been happier. Not even sitting in the cockpit of a plane brought this level of happiness. Well, maybe the first time, but not this. This was different.

They reached the gate and the next few minutes were spent finding their seats.

Sierra looked at the program, then took in everything around her.

She didn't seem interested in conversation, so he let her sit quietly.

CHAPTER 44

*S*ierra sat next to Mike, the sounds of the orchestra washing over her.

She tuned out the hushed conversations around them. If she closed her eyes, she could imagine being on the stage. Preparing for a performance.

She imagined what the musicians must feel. Their excitement. Their anticipation. their nervousness.

Then she'd catch a whiff of Mike's cologne and she'd be back to a completely different amazing world.

Mike had brought her here. Sierra couldn't think of anywhere he could have brought her on this Christmas Eve that could have even come close to more perfect.

The orchestra.

That was Sierra's secret dream. She was enrolled, in fact, to start music classes in January at the university in Madison. She'd had other offers, too, but Madison had seemed to make the most sense. Either way, she was even more determined now than she had been before.

She knew it made no sense to start classes now. Now when she was pregnant of all things.

But the pregnancy had turned her life around.

Made her want to start her life over again. To do it right.

And music was her passion.

That was one of the things she'd learned from hanging around pilots through her sister and work. Every pilot she knew followed his dream. Or her dream as the case may be.

And often times they did it with very little if any family support.

It was especially difficult for those who went off on their own. Like Mike. Even in today's world, it was hard for people to see the point of taking chances. Of doing something out of the norm.

Even if Sierra told her parents that she was going back to school, they'd be excited. Until she told them she was majoring in music. Then they'd tell her she was wasting her time and money.

Do it as a hobby, they'd say. *Get a real job. That pays you a salary. And benefits.*

Sierra didn't even bother telling them.

She didn't even tell her sister. And Wynter was the one person who would be supportive of anything she did.

To a point anyway. Now that Sierra was having a baby. On her own. She would be hard pressed to find anyone who would be willing to stand behind her. And mean it.

But here, right in front of her was the dream.

She turned and looked into Mike's eyes. Leaned over to whisper in his ear. "Thank you."

He grinned. "You like?"

"Like?" She grinned back. "It's the best possible gift."

He put a finger under her chin and kissed her. "Good to know." His breath was soft against her lips. "I guess I made a lucky guess."

"You have no idea."

Between the orchestra and Mike, she was in heavenly bliss.

And now was even more determined to make music a part of her life.

CHAPTER 45

Two weeks later

Mike dropped his landing gear on the Cessna and prepared for landing.

He'd always felt most at home in the air. The air was where he had time to think. To let his thoughts wander where they would.

He'd flown so many hours, the flying part was second nature. Automatic even.

It had been two weeks and two days since Christmas. Two weeks since he'd dropped Sierra off at her apartment.

If he closed his eyes, he could still smell her lavender soap mixed with the crisp cold snow fall from the day he'd dropped her off in Madison.

They'd lingered over lunch at a local pizza place, but he knew he had to leave.

He also knew he'd be back.

There were so many things they hadn't talked about. He wanted to know everything about her. Her plans. But he forced himself to live in the moment.

That was a hard -learned lesson. Focus on the now, for tomorrow may never come.

A smooth landing put his thoughts back on the present. Like a few other pilots, he'd talked to, he kept his deep, philosophical thoughts for the air and once he landed, he planted his thoughts back on real-world issues.

This was the first time he'd been back close-enough to Madison to see Sierra, so tonight was the night.

He hadn't called her. Or even texted even though they had each other's numbers.

He was giving her some time to herself and he was getting his own thoughts and plans together.

And, besides, he'd been booked solid, giving him plenty of air time.

Instead of taking an airport car, he rented a car.

He was planning to be in Madison for several days.

He had something he wanted to talk to Sierra about.

Humming to the music, he hopped on the freeway and headed to Sierra's apartment.

Snowflakes were falling like a slow drizzle. Maybe they would get lucky and the airport would close down for a few days.

He turned into her apartment complex and parked in front of her door. Something looked different. He double-checked the number, but he was in the right place.

After knocking on the door, he waited about three minutes, then knocked again. And again.

The neighbor, a young mother with a baby on her hip, came out her door. "Are you looking for Sierra?"

"Yes," Mike twirled to face the young mother, relieved that he was in the right place. "I hope I didn't disturb you." Sierra had introduced them a couple of weeks ago in passing.

"Not at all." She shifted the baby with one arm and ran a

hand through her hair with the other. "It's been a rough day of fit throwing."

"Good," Mike said. "Is she home? Sierra?"

"Oh. No. Actually she left three days ago."

"Left? What do you mean?" She couldn't just up and leave. Could she?

"Packed up her car and left."

Mike looked back at the door. There had been a plant… or something. That's why it looked different. "Is she coming back?"

"I don't think so. There's a new tenant moving in tomorrow."

Mike put both hands on his hips. "Where did she go?"

"She said something about going off to college."

"In Madison. Why would she move?"

The baby cooed. "I'm sorry. I really need to feed him before he throws another fit."

"It's ok. Just tell me. Where did she go?"

"She didn't tell me. But she did say something about Pittsburgh or Philadelphia, I think."

Mike looked blankly at her, then turned, mumbled something in the form of a thank you and walked back to his car.

"Hope that helps," the girl said as he got back into his car.

The first thing Mike did was call Sierra's number. He wasn't going to be silly about this.

The number you have dialed is no longer in service.

CHAPTER 46

*S*ierra straightened the stack of textbooks on her new desk from Target. She had everything ready. Books. Computer. Notebooks. Pens. Even a new book sack with Duquesne University written on it. Everything smelled new.

She popped a cinnamon mint in her mouth to help with the dryness.

She sat in her desk chair – new also – and looked out the window. It was snowing. And the snow reminded her of New York.

Thinking about New York brought back the feelings of sadness. Memories of Mike and their Christmas Eve date.

Walking along Times Square with Mike. Sitting in Lincoln Center with classical music flowing all around, seeping into her bones.

Even when she thought about the hospital, it brought memories of Mike and the way he'd been there for her. Holding her hand.

Duquesne University in Pittsburgh.

One of the best music schools in the country. Sierra had

applied there last fall on a whim. She never once thought she had a chance of actually being accepted.

When she'd gotten home from New York – and her sister's wedding – she'd had a letter from them.

She'd tacked it to her refrigerator right next to the letter from the University of Wisconsin- Madison. For a week, she'd studied the letters. Thought about her options.

While she waited for Mike to call.

Madison was the easy choice out of the two.

Duquesne was the difficult choice. The grand gesture.

She knew that going to college while having an infant, not to mention the whole pregnancy and birth part of it, but moving across the country to a new place to do it?

Even she admitted that was insane.

Plus, she had Mike to think about.

She was so in love with him, she could barely see straight.

After about five days, she decided it was a good thing he didn't call. He clouded her judgement. There was just no other way to put it.

She couldn't help wondering what he would think.

She hadn't told him about it. Her dream of being a musician. That was still her own private thing. She still hadn't even told Wynter. Fortunately Wynter was still in honeymoon bliss and wasn't concerned about her sister.

All the better. Sierra wasn't in a place to explain something she didn't understand.

She'd taken walks in the cold. In the snow.

She'd watched television. She'd read.

She'd listened to music. Classical music.

Finally, she'd gone to the Madison University campus and walked around. It just didn't feel right.

She kept thinking about the letter from Pittsburgh. She wanted to do it right this time.

After all the screw ups she'd made, she wanted a fresh start.

And somehow Madison didn't feel like a fresh start. Not even adding in the university.

She couldn't reinvent herself by living in the same old apartment. In the same city. Driving along the same roads.

She needed to blow up her world and start again.

So she'd packed her stuff. Her clothes and personal items. A box of photographs. She'd donated everything else to charity.

Today, she decided, she'd go shopping. A new life called for new clothes. She was going to look around for a new style. Now that she was going to be a mother and student, it was time for a fashion overall.

She took a deep ragged breath.

She needed to let Wynter know that she'd moved.

Eventually.

The only thing she was keeping, really, was her cell phone number. And to be honest with herself, she hadn't completely decided whether or not to get that changed.

So for a little test, she'd turned her phone on airplane mode. The only person who might need her was Wynter. So every morning when she woke up she checked for messages and again every night.

So far, it was working out quite nicely. She didn't have to explain herself to anyone.

She'd gotten a job as a student worker, but that job didn't start until next week. So she still had a little more time to get everything ready.

She wanted to hit the ground running as they said. Wanted to have everything in place before classes started.

But Mike hadn't called. And the longer he didn't call, the more she realized that her three days with him had been one of those once in life time fantasies.

She opened her phone and looked at the photo of them together that night at the orchestra. Her wearing the most beautiful burgundy dress and him wearing a black tux.

Just looking at the photo brought a lump to her throat. They made a beautiful, happy couple. His arms were around her and they were both grinning like loons.

Her finger hovered over the delete button. She could forever send this visual memory of their time together away.

And really get on with her life.

But after a few seconds, she realized she didn't want to do it. She wanted to keep the photo. To remember that true love did exist. That she was capable.

And someday after the baby was old enough, she'd entertain the notion of dating again.

Of possibly bringing a man into their lives.

Maybe.

But right now she had her life to get into order.

CHAPTER 47

$\mathcal{M}$ike drove around Madison in a daze. He didn't know what to do.

He hadn't contacted Sierra because he wanted to give her some space.

But in truth, he knew that was merely a flimsy excuse. He wanted to get his own plans in order. To make sure he was prepared for what he was going to do.

Taking on a wife and baby was not a small thing.

He needed some air time to make sure he wasn't making the decision based on a whim. Or an old fantasy.

He'd come to the conclusion that it wasn't a whim and, though it had been a fantasy come to life, he wanted to bring it home. To make it real.

He was ready. He was ready to be a husband and father.

He was in love with Sierra and he couldn't bear to be apart from her any more. Sure, he'd still fly. But at night he'd be home with her. If he had to go on an overnight trip, they'd figure that out together.

He wasn't going to make all their plans himself. He wanted her in there with him. A partner.

He should have stayed in touch with her. Sierra wasn't the kind of girl who sat around waiting on a man to call.

She probably assumed that the persona he presented to the world was true. That he was a love 'em and leave 'em kind of guy.

Couldn't be farther from the truth. Sure, he'd done it, but who hadn't.

But not when he loved the girl.

And he loved this girl.

He needed to think. He pulled into the first bar he came to and went inside. Ordered a martini, dirty, extra olives.

As was his nature, he didn't drink it. He wasn't sure when he'd be flying again. If there was a storm coming, he didn't want to get stuck in Madison. Not if Sierra wasn't here.

He picked up a napkin and pen and began to write down his thoughts. He wrote *Pennsylvania* at the top. Added the word *college.*

Had Sierra even gone to undergrad? He ran a hand through his hair. He didn't even know. He hadn't asked her questions that didn't matter. Questions with answers that wouldn't change anything.

Between Pittsburgh and Philadelphia, there were tons of colleges she could be going to. Too many to go off blindly searching.

She could have gone straight there or she could have gone somewhere else in the meantime. Her parents?

He wrote down *parents* and crossed it off. They weren't close. More like estranged. So she wouldn't go there.

Her sister. Wynter. He wrote down *Wynter* and took a sip of his martini.

Wynter's husband was Mike's best friend. He could call Bradford. If Bradford didn't know where Sierra was, he could find out.

Sierra and Wynter were close, so Wynter would know.

She might not want to tell him, especially if Mike had accidentally hurt Sierra. But he could make it right.

If he could just find Sierra, he could fix it.

He pulled out his cell phone and dialed Bradford's number.

Fifteen minutes later, he'd incited a panic in the entire Jordan family.

No one knew where Sierra was.

And Sierra wasn't answering her phone.

CHAPTER 48

After a warm bath, Sierra made a hot cup of tea and settled into the big comfy chair she'd placed in front of the patio window.

It was snowing now. Fat, Fluffy flakes.

Someone down the hall was cooking something that smelled like bacon, but she didn't mind. She was past the nausea phase of her pregnancy.

Thank goodness.

She'd often wondered if she was going to survive that part.

Then she turned on her cell phone.

Fifty-seven text messages. Sixteen voice messages.

She knew from the first message that they had somehow found out she'd moved.

How did that happen?

Wynter was in honeymoon bliss and had no plans to visit. Her parents never came to visit. That wasn't even a possibility.

It didn't take long to figure out what had happened.

Sierra was stunned.

Mike had come looking for her.

She only knew this through her sister's messages. Mike hadn't left a message. Or a text. There was no way to know how many times he'd actually called. At least once if her sister's messages were any indication.

She played every message, each one more frantic than the first. In the first message, Wynter sounded skeptical. Like maybe Mike got it wrong. Then the messages moved to confused. All the way through to panicked.

By later afternoon, Wynter had actually shown up at her old apartment.

The text messages were about the same. Apparently Wynter thought that maybe even if she didn't answer the phone, she'd see the messages.

After she'd gone through all the messages, Sierra put her phone in her lap.

Ok. She should have told *someone*. That someone should have been Wynter. As Wynter said in one of her messages. *You don't get to do this. We're family. Besides, you're pregnant. And you've had some complications.*

Sierra took a sip of tea, but it had gone cold. She made a face and set it aside.

Well, now she had some explaining to do whether she wanted to or not.

Sierra knew she couldn't have it both ways. She couldn't have complete freedom and have people who cared about her.

And truthfully, she wasn't trying to disappear. She just wanted to get started on changes before people started discouraging her.

She'd been afraid to tell Wynter she was moving to Pittsburgh. Wynter would have talked her out of it. She'd say it wasn't a good time. There was the baby coming and all.

She was right, of course.

But Sierra didn't want to be talked out of it. She wanted to be successful at her metamorphosis.

And Wynter was the one person who could change her mind.

As far as Mike went, she didn't quite know what to think about that.

She got up and heated some more water for tea. There was nothing worse than cold tea.

Fortified with a fresh cup of hot tea, she sat back in her chair to think. About Mike.

But her phone rang.

It was Wynter.

CHAPTER 49

$\mathcal{M}$ ike spent the night in Madison at a hotel.

It was the sanest thing he could think to do. If he got in his plane, he'd just end up in Pittsburgh or Philadelphia.

So he decided to just hold tight. To wait.

He didn't have to wait long. Wynter found her.

In Pittsburgh.

That's all he knew for now.

Sierra was safe. But she had indeed moved to Pittsburgh. Without telling anyone.

Mike made his way to the hotel bar.

It was snowing outside and the airport was closed. He was pretty safe in having a drink. Wouldn't be any flying in the foreseeable future.

He ordered a martini again, but again, he didn't drink it. One sip only.

He just couldn't figure out why she didn't tell him.

You didn't call. You didn't text. You just ignored her.

Right. Mike had treated her the same way he'd treat a girl he wasn't interested in.

Damn, but bad habits were hard to break.

He knew one thing.

This was the last time he'd ever take Sierra for granted. Even a little.

That is if she was still talking to him.

He really couldn't blame her if she wasn't.

When they were in New York, had she known she was moving? That she was going back to college?

She made no mention of it whatsoever.

He couldn't help but to find that strange.

But maybe she hadn't decided yet. Maybe when she didn't hear from him, it had tipped her over the edge into leaving.

But she hadn't even told her sister.

She did what she needed to do. He certainly wasn't one to judge. He'd done some things that people thought were crazy a time or two. And look at where he was now.

If he hadn't done those *crazy* things, he would certainly not be a successful pilot, much less a successful business owner.

He had enough money that he could stop work now and live more than comfortably for the rest of his life without ever flying again.

But he loved flying. Loved - loved - flying. More than anything.

Maybe Sierra was pursuing her passion.

The thought of anyone, even her family, trying to discourage her had his blood boiling. But he tamped it down. It wasn't his place to get in on family business.

He could even see their point. Sierra was pregnant. Her life was about to get way more difficult.

But what her family didn't know was that Sierra now had him with her. She didn't have to go it alone.

If... Big if.

If she wanted him.

CHAPTER 50

"Mike's looking for you." Wynter's voice was a little perplexed.

"Why?" Sierra had no intention of satisfying her sister's curiosity about why her husband's best friend would be looking for her. It had to be driving her crazy. Not knowing.

She had Wynter on speaker phone and moved about the kitchen while she threw together a salad.

"I was hoping you could tell me." Wynter stopped. Waited.

"I don't know. I saw him at the wedding." Sierra kept her voice unconcerned as she peeled an avocado.

"He knows… knew… where you live."

"He took me home after the wedding." She added some cherry tomatoes to her bowl.

"Was something wrong with your car?"

"No," Sierra said, as though she hadn't a concern in the world. "I wasn't feeling well." Maybe she should go into acting.

"Oh," Wynter said, then muttered to herself. "Well, that make sense. He is Bradford's good friend. And we weren't there."

Sierra smiled to herself. Sometimes Wynter was so easily distracted. But then her own curiosity got the best of her. "Did he say what he wanted with me?" She bit her lip as she sprinkled some bacon bits on her salad.

"He just said he was worried. That he went to your apartment and you weren't there. He said he hadn't seen you since the day after Christmas."

Sierra took her salad and phone and went to sit in her favorite comfy chair by the window. So much for keeping things from her sister.

Mike pretty much told her there was something going on between them. Even though there wasn't. Was there? "Is that all he said?" Geez. She felt like they were back in grade school.

She should just call Mike and tell him where she was.

"That's all he said. Just asked me to please let him know that you were ok."

Sierra huffed out a breath. That was so not helpful. She still didn't know what he wanted with her.

How could he go all this long? Two whole weeks and expect her to be there waiting for her when he decided to show up.

She laughed at herself.

"What's funny?" Wynter asked.

"Nothing." Her phone chimed indicating a text message. She glanced at it. "I have to go."

She hung up the phone and opened the text message from Mike.

First, sorry about telling Wynter. I didn't know what to do when your neighbor said you moved. I was worried. So... if you get this, can we meet? Somewhere? I really need to talk to you.

Sierra set her phone aside and pressed her fingertips against her eyes. So he was all into her at her sister's wedding and in New York. Then he just disappears and expects her to be just waiting around for him?

Well, that's not how it works.

CHAPTER 51

ike fell asleep in the hotel bed with his phone in his hand.

His message to Sierra said it was delivered almost immediately.

But no response.

The morning sunlight streamed over his face. He never slept this late. It was almost eight o'clock.

He sat up, checked his messages. Still no response from Sierra. No other messages from Wynter. No phone calls.

He stepped into the shower. Outside of flying, it was where he did his best thinking.

Ok, he thought. He'd put the ball in her court. If she didn't want to respond, he had to leave her alone.

He wasn't about to insist that someone interact with him.

If she didn't want to talk to him, she certainly didn't have to. It would break his heart, but he understood.

She had a lot going on in her life right now.

But adding school to it?

He shook his head. He'd never known anyone like Sierra

Jordan. She was the bravest, most beautiful woman he'd ever known.

He loved her, so he had to let her go.

When he got out of the shower, he had a text message from Sierra.

Meet me at Heinz Hall at 6:30. You can pick up your ticket at the booth.

Mike grinned, slipped on his clothes, and checked the weather, all in one smooth movement.

He was flying today after all.

CHAPTER 52

Sierra sat in her seat on the Main Floor of Heinz Hall in Pittsburgh. She'd reserved the last two seats available for tonight's symphony.

The concert hall was absolutely stunning in ornamental gold décor on the walls and red seats. Already the musicians were warming up behind the curtain, filling the huge open building with sounds of things to come.

She adjusted her burgundy skirt with its sparkly sequins that flowed from the waist down the front of the skirt.

She couldn't decide if she was more excited about seeing Mike – if he showed up – or being here for the symphony.

She'd decided to tell him her crazy plan about getting a music degree and learning to play an instrument. And she'd decided that the best place to do that was here. Right here where she wanted to perform some day.

He would understand. He had to. He was a pilot. With his own very successful business. He'd taken risks.

It shouldn't matter that she'd started a few years later than most people and that she was about to be a single mom.

Obstacles were there to be overcome.

Hence, her grand gesture.

A reset for her life.

She didn't know what Mike wanted from her. She didn't know if he just wanted to continue their friendship or if he wanted something more.

She wasn't even sure what she wanted.

She checked the time on her phone. Mike should be here any minute now. It was six twenty.

No. She wasn't being completely truthful with herself.

She knew what she wanted. She just wasn't sure that Mike had it to offer.

She wanted a life with him. But Mike wasn't a family man. He never had been.

He'd always been footloose and fancy free.

Perhaps that was one of the things that attracted her to him. Perhaps she wanted a similar lifestyle for herself.

Optimal word being *wanted.* It may have been a lifestyle she'd wanted and maybe even had for herself at one time.

But not anymore. Now that she was pregnant and starting over, she wanted stability. And if Mike wasn't willing or able to offer that, he could be the baby's "uncle" and see him on occasion.

Sierra straightened in her chair and lifted her chin. If that was how it had to be, then that was just how it had to be.

She didn't expect anyone to be interested in being involved in her new lifestyle.

But she did want to explain to Mike what she was doing. She felt she owed him that much. He'd been a good friend in her time of need more than once.

CHAPTER 53

When Mike spotted Sierra sitting in the seat next to the one on his assigned ticket, he was immediately struck by her strength.

She sat straight in her seat, her chin held high.

She was wearing the dress he'd bought for her in New York. It brought a lump to his throat. She'd moved across the country and not only brought the dress with her, but she'd worn it. For him.

Her hair was down, pulled over one shoulder in a long soft curl.

Though her expression was wistful, her skin was glowing.

He made his way past the other people taking their seats and moving about.

She didn't notice him until he was standing next to her.

She looked up and smiled.

Just looking at her made his heart swell. She looked so calm. So serene.

So full of life and youth.

He wanted to know about whatever it was that prompted her to pick up and move to this new city. He hoped that she was moving toward something and not running away from something.

If she was going toward something, he could help her, but if she was running away from something…. Well…. Maybe he could help with that, too, but it might be a bit harder. It depended on what it was.

If it was her family, he'd prefer not to get involved. Old boyfriend, again, prefer not to get involved.

"You're beautiful," he said, sliding into the chair next to hers.

She smiled. "So are you."

"Then we make a good couple, don't we?" Not something he'd planned on saying. He didn't want to frighten her. But he wanted her to know that he wanted more than just friendship.

Mike had plenty of friends. He didn't need any more.

"You're a hard person to track down."

She smiled softly. "I didn't know I needed tracking down."

"I was just giving you some space." He kept his eyes on hers. Now was the time to be truthful.

"I've got plenty of space." Her green eyes sparkled. "I don't need any more."

She was the woman after his heart.

If ever there was a woman who'd been custom made just for him, Mike knew it was Sierra Jordan.

All a man could do when he found the woman who'd been made for him was hope and pray that she felt the same. As far as he knew, there was no guarantee that the two had to match up.

But she'd invited him here. And that was something he could grab hold to. That was something he could work with.

And when it came to Sierra Jordan, he was willing to put in the work.

"I promise to never give you space again."

She laughed. And some of the tension was broken.

Conversation and laughter swirled around them. The musicians were warming up. Mike liked this part of a symphony better than the actual performance.

Conversations were allowed with unobtrusive music in the background. There was an air of anticipation in the air.

"This is nice," he said. It took all his restraint to not jump in. To ask her the purpose of her invitation. And he used the word invitation loosely. She hadn't really asked, had she?

She looked into his eyes. And he saw unshed tears.

Something was wrong. His mind immediately jumped to all sorts of possibilities. The baby. Or perhaps she didn't want to see him anymore.

Though it was certainly a long way to bring him just to tell him she didn't want to see him anymore.

But Sierra knew that Mike loved to fly. Any excuse, he always said.

Then there were the symphony tickets. That was no small expense for her.

"Something's wrong," he said.

She shook her head and looked around. "This is beautiful, isn't it?"

"Very." But he kept his eyes on her.

She took a deep breath and turned back to him. "I didn't tell you before, but I'm going back to college." She shrugged. "Well *to* college, since I never went before. It can't really be going *back*."

He nodded. "That's wonderful."

"You knew." She sounded a bit disappointed.

He grinned. "Sorry, but yes. Wynter told me."

"Well then." She sat back in her seat and stared straight ahead.

"That's why you wanted to talk to me. To tell me that?"

She looked at him sideways. "I know. I could have told

you on the phone. Instead of bringing you all the way out here."

"I wanted to see you anyway." He grinned. "So thank you."

She nodded. And didn't seem to quite know what to say next.

"Wynter seemed surprised," he said. "that you came all the way out here instead of going to school in Madison."

"It's no different," she said, a tinge of anger in her voice. "Wynter's in Cassville now. And my parents don't have anything to do with me. I don't see why everyone's so worried about where I live."

"Mike held up a hand. You're talking to the choir here. You can live anywhere you want to live."

She blew out a breath. "I'm sorry. You haven't done anything. I just feel like everyone is judging me."

They leaned back to make space for another couple to move past them to take their own seats.

"Judge? Why? What you're doing is commendable. I've so very proud of you for going to college."

"Well," she said, glancing at him out of the corner of her eyes. "It's not exactly the whole story. That's why I wanted you to come here. Tonight."

He leaned forward. "Sounds mysterious. Tell me."

She plunged right in. Finally. "I'm going to study music. I want to learn an instrument." She nodded toward the stage. "I want to perform. I want to be a musician."

Mike had not been expecting this. He made a conscious effort to make sure his face didn't show the shock that he was feeling inside.

He'd thought she'd study something like psychology. That would fit her troubled past. But music? He had no idea.

She looked down. Toyed with her program. "See. Even you don't understand."

"No, I..." He self-corrected his reaction. People had

reacted to him in a similar way when he'd began announcing his desire to fly airplanes. "I'm just caught off guard. It's not at all what I expected."

She looked so sad. So lost.

So disappointed.

She'd expected him of all people to support her.

And he did. He would. As soon as he wrapped his head around it.

"You'll be wonderful," he said. He pictured her sitting up front. Playing an instrument. She'd be beautiful. "What instrument do you want to play?"

"I don't know yet. I have some exploring to do."

"Is that how it works?"

"I don't know. I hope so." She looked at him, her face bright again as she talked about this. "I played the clarinet in junior high for a minute. But I don't think that's the one for me. Maybe the cello."

"I'm sure you'll have the opportunity to try out different ones."

"That's my plan."

"So that's it?" he asked, leaning back in his chair again. "You were worried that people wouldn't support you in studying performing arts?"

"Yes. It's not something that leads to a *good* job with benefits and whatnot." She swept a hand over her abdomen. "Especially not with a child on the way."

"Right," he said, scrubbing his chin. "I guess people would have a hard time understanding that."

She looked up. "That's why I didn't tell anyone."

"I'm sure it won't be easy."

Her chin quivered a bit. "But it can be done. Right?"

He took her hands and locked his gaze onto hers. "Sierra. You can do anything you choose to do. What other people think has absolutely nothing to do with what you can do."

"But there's the baby."

So even though she'd made her decision, she wasn't sure how she was going to make it happen.

She was afraid.

"That doesn't matter either. That's what day care is for."

"Right." She held her chin up. "I can do this, can't I?"

He ran a hand along the curl that fell to her shoulder. So soft.

He loved that she allowed him to see her vulnerable side. He liked her toughness, but he also liked that she had a softer side.

Hell, he liked everything about her.

And if she wanted to play a musical instrument and perform in front of hundreds of people, he would do everything in his power to help her make that happen.

Besides, he'd planned on helping her out anyway. Maybe this was a good time to bring that up.

He wiped his damp palms on the slacks of his tux.

CHAPTER 54

Mike seemed nervous about something.

Sierra opened her program, then closed it without seeing the words written on it.

The lights would be dimming before long and they'd have to stop talking.

The musicians were quiet now behind the curtain. The people sitting around them were talking in hushed tones in anticipation of the performance starting.

It was almost time.

"Sierra," Mike said, then waited until he had her attention. "You've always been special to me."

She smiled. "And you to me."

"Oh hell," he said, running a hand through his hair. Then he took her hands in his.

And slid out of his seat onto one knee. He gently pressed his lips against her knuckles and looked into her eyes.

Sierra gasped. What was he doing?

Everyone around them had gone quiet. Maybe the performance was about to start. "What are you doing?" she asked.

Then he just blurted out "Will you marry me?"

Sierra's mouth dropped open. Then she squeezed her eyes tightly closed. She was imagining things.

But when she opened her eyes, he was still there. Smiling a nervous, lopsided grin. "Will you marry me? And live happily ever after with me?"

Mike Phillips didn't do happily ever after. He didn't do marriage.

She glanced around. People were watching them.

"The baby," she whispered.

He grinned. "Ours."

"Are you sure you mean this?"

A flash of hurt crossed his features.

He did mean it.

"Yes," she said quickly. "Yes. Yes."

Then she was in his arms.

And everyone around them clapped.

Her first performance.

EPILOGUE

Three weeks later

 $\mathcal{S}$ ierra and Mike sat cuddled on her little sofa. They were wearing warm comfortable sweat pants.

And it was snowing outside. Two days straight, leaving the world tucked beneath a white blanket. Big, fluffy flakes.

Sierra admired the sparkly Tiffany diamond ring on her finger as she shared a bowl of popcorn with Mike.

They'd been married two days after his proposal.

They both agreed there was no need to wait. And every reason to have it done. She was married before classes started and definitely before the baby came.

They went to a local justice of the peace. Nothing fancy.

They flew to Cassville the next day to tell Wynter and Bradford.

Needless to say, Wynter wasn't happy about missing her sister's wedding, but she seemed to understand enough to be happy for Sierra. Happy, but obviously perplexed about how this could happen.

No one knew. No one could have known that Sierra and

Mike had been crushing on each other since Sierra was a teen.

Right now they were watching a Hallmark movie.

By the time they got to the last fifteen minutes and everything seemed lost, Sierra had tears streaming down her cheeks. "There's no way they can fix this," she said, wiping her eyes.

"Of course they can." Mike hugged her close, kissing her ear lobe.

"I just don't see a way for them to get together."

He chuckled. "There's always a way. True love can overcome anything. Just look at us."

Sierra laughed through her tears. "I guess you're right."

"Of course I am. I have experience in these matters."

And then, just like Mike said, the couple found a way and the movie ended with a happily ever after.

Sierra didn't want to move. She wanted to stay in Mike's arms forever.

He was the love of her life.

And for once, things had worked out perfectly.

ANOTHER EPILOGUE

Mike handed the tiny infant over to Sierra. They were both smiling like loons.

Though he had to admit, he'd never seen his wife look so exhausted. The birth had taken three hours, but it had seemed like forever. The doctor said it was amazingly fast for a first baby.

The nurse had handed Phil – appropriately named for Mike's last name and the Philharmonic symphony – to Mike just minutes after he was born.

Mike's body must have released a flood of oxytocin because he'd never felt such an overwhelming sense of pure joy and love.

It was different from the way he felt about Sierra. With Phil, he felt pure protection.

And he'd been right. It hadn't mattered one bit that he wasn't the biological father. But already, he and Sierra were making plans for her to have a second baby. With Mike as the father, of course.

"Look," Sierra said. "Look at his tiny little toes."

Mike counted them. Again. It was fascinating how a baby could come out so perfectly. "They're all there. Ten toes and ten little fingers."

"He's perfect."

"He is. He'll be playing the cello just like his mom in no time."

"You never know," she said, pressing her cheek against the baby's head. "He might want to be a pilot like his daddy."

His daddy.

He was a daddy.

Mike blinked back the moisture that formed in his eyes.

Somehow his life turned around so fast in the last few months.

Sierra had saved him from himself. From a meaningless life.

His life had meaning now.

The baby cried and Sierra rocked him gently.

So much meaning. More meaning than any one man deserved.

Someone knocked on the door. "Flower delivery."

Mike took the bouquet that included a white teddy bear and brought the card with him back to Sierra's side.

"Who's it from?"

He studied the card. "It's from Noah and Savannah."

So many happy and wonder-filled times ahead for you. Congratulations! You two are going to make such amazing parents!

Mike read the card out loud. "We are, aren't we?" he said. "We're going to be amazing parents."

Then he kissed Sierra on the mouth.

Anything he did with Sierra was going to be amazing.

She was the love of his life.

He was besotted.

Want to read more second chance romance? How about a bonus short story?

GET MY BONUS SHORT STORY
https://BookHip.com/XBFBPAA

Keep reading for a preview of *Just Happened...* the next sweet wholesome story in the *For the Love of the Flight Series...*

KATHRYN KALEIGH
Just Happened
FOR THE LOVE OF THE FLIGHT

JUST HAPPENED — PREVIEW

CHAPTER 1

Annabelle Lawson put the cap on her thick highlighter and huffed out a breath at the long yellow streak across the paper. She would have to print a fresh copy when she got to the hotel. She leaned back in the leather seat and braced herself for the next air pocket. There was never just one.

She stared out at the checkerboard of fields below and wondered who the new pilot was. It seemed like every time she flew with Skye Travels Noah had hired someone new. His company was growing like gangbusters, seemingly with little effort on his part.

Of course, Annabelle knew firsthand that a company never grew without considerable effort.

Unfortunately, hers was suffering. A new medical waste removal company had come into Houston and had all but shut Steri-Waste down. Annabelle didn't care so much about the company, but it had been started by her grandfather, Nathaniel, so she was determined to save it. Besides, Steri-Waste had funded her college and kept her from having to worry about money.

The plane dipped into the inevitable air pocket and Annabelle gasped. She preferred flying with Samuel, but he worked with Noah at Skye Travels now. So she now flew with Skye Travels. Unfortunately, Samuel was out with the birth of his first child, so Annabelle had been forced to fly with another pilot.

Noah assured her that he was top-notch, but she was having doubts. Samuel always went around the turbulent weather. She closed her eyes. In all fairness, she knew that wasn't always possible. She was just miffed at having to fly with someone new. She'd met the copilot, Beau, but she'd yet to meet her pilot. In fact, from her seat, she could see Beau, but not her pilot.

She really just wanted to get this meeting over with. Over and done. She'd read all the paperwork, had her attorney double-check the contract, and was ready to just sign and get on with other things. Steri-Waste kept her at her standard of living, but more importantly her mother relied on the income. Her parents' divorce had been bad. The brutal divorce coupled with her father's floundering oil company, had left her mother relying on the Steri-Waste income. Unfortunately, it wasn't something that held Annabelle's interest.

But as executor of her grandfather's estate, it was just one of her many responsibilities.

She was anxious to get started on next venture – a publishing business. Publishing was something she could get excited about. Medical waste. Not so much.

Chapter 2

Brandon Barrett made a swing around Mackinac Island for his own pleasure. He'd heard so much about the island.

Somewhere in Time was his sister's favorite movie of all time and she'd spent her honeymoon on the island during some kind of *Somewhere in Time* festival. He didn't know the details, but his sister was intrigued as was her new husband.

He hit the Mackinac Island Airport runway at a perfect angle if he did have to say so himself. It was a short runway to begin with and the plane barely squeezed within the limits the runway could handle.

Feeling rather pleased with himself, he got up to see what kind of passengers he had on board. He'd already been in cockpit when they came in and his copilot, Beau, was taking care of everything in the back.

He stood up, stretched, and turned around to the empty cabin. Surely he didn't fly all the way up here with no passengers. Beau hadn't said much, but both of them were preoccupied with their own things. He went to the door and was about to call out to Beau.

Then he heard someone moving about.

He turned and saw her standing up and moving into the aisle.

His heart rate ramped up to full force. She was the most beautiful creature he'd ever seen.

She wasn't smiling. In fact, when she looked up and saw him, she scowled.

He'd just made an amazing landing and she wasn't showing any signs of being grateful. None whatsoever.

She put her handbag strap over her head and gathered up her leather briefcase. She was wearing a charcoal gray skirt and matching jacket. She had on a forest green blouse beneath it. As she walked toward him, he saw that she wore a silver chain that sparked with about four tiny diamonds around her neck and diamond studs on her earlobes. Her blonde-highlighted hair was loosely swept off her face. He also noticed that instead of the traditional business heels, she wore flat lace up booties.

One of the side effects of having a sister was learning to notice such details. As she neared him, he noticed a light scent of sandalwood and gardenia. His stomach clutched as he became acutely aware of her delicate femininity.

He smiled and asked his standard question. "How was your flight?"

"Rather bumpy, don't you think?" She gave him a half smile as she walked past him. Beau was there to help her down the steep steps to the ground.

Brandon rolled his eyes. She really knew how to crush a man's ego.

As he watched her walk toward the waiting car, he smiled.

Beauty with an edge.

Keep Reading Just Happened...

ALSO BY KATHRYN KALEIGH

For a full and up-to-date list of Kathryn Kaleigh's books, visit
www.kathrynkaleigh.com

MAGNETIC NORTH

Sexy Contemporary Romance

The Worthington Family

Second Chance Kisses

Second Chance Secrets

First Time Charm

Three Broken Rules

Second Chance Destiny

Unexpected Vows

FOR THE LOVE OF THE FLIGHT

Sweet, Wholesome Contemporary Romance

The Worthington Family

Begin Again

Love Again

Falling Again

Just Stay

Just Chance

Just Believe

Just Us

Just Once

Just Happened

Just Maybe

Just Pretend

Just Because

ROMANTIC SUSPENSE COLLECTION

Serenity

Lost and Found

Courting Alley Cat

All I Want for Christmas

FATED MATES SEXY ROMANCE

Riley's Mate

Aiden's Mate

Brayden's Mate

INTO THE MIST
Time Travel Romance
The Becquerel Family

Written in the Wind

Scripted in the Stars

Destined in the Twilight

Promised in the Mist

Trapped in the Melody

TIME SPELLS BECKON

Time Travel Romance

The Becquerel Family

Twist of Fate

When the Stars Align

Once in a Blue Moon

Once Upon a Christmas

A Wish Upon a Star

Storm Spells Beckon

Time Travel Romance

The Becquerel Family

When Lightning Strikes

Storm of Time

Midnight Storm

When the Moon Falls

Stormborn Angel

Time Tempest

The Heart Remembers

A Moment in Time

Moonlight Shadows

Standalone Time Travel

Rescued in Time

Falling Through to Forever

HISTORICAL WESTERN ROMANCE
Sweet, American Historical Romance

Finding Natalie

Promising Samantha

Falling for Allyson

Saving Savannah

Claiming Charlie

Rescuing Kiera

Protecting Gabriella

Courting Isabella

HISTORICAL ROMANCE
Sweet American Historical Romance

Jasmine Kisses

Magnolia Kisses

Gardenia Kisses

Love Always

Beyond Enemy Lines

Hearts Under Siege

Hearts Under Fire

Wait for Me

Take Me Home

Keep Me Safe

Away Down South in Dixie

The Reluctant Bride

Sign up for my newsletter at www.kathrynkaleigh.com to be the first to hear about new releases, as well as exclusive content, and more!

www.ingramcontent.com/pod-product-compliance
Lightning Source LLC
Chambersburg PA
CBHW031136130726
47988CB00006B/2394